SATAN'S
CHILDREN

"Those with no sides and no causes. Those who won't take measure of their own strength, for fear of antagonizing their own weakness. Those who don't like to make waves — or enemies. Those for whom freedom, honour, truth, and principles are only literature. Those who live small, love small - die small. It's the reductionist approach to life: if you keep it small, you'll keep it under control. If you don't make any noise, the bogeyman won't find you. But it's all an illusion, because they die too, those people who roll up their spirits into tiny little balls so as to be safe. Safe? From what? Life is always on the edge of death; narrow streets lead to the same place as wide avenues, and a little candle burns itself out just like a flaming torch does. I choose my own way to burn."

– Sophie Scholl (German student and and anti-fascist freedom fighter, born 9 May 1921, executed by the Nazis 22 February 1943).

CONTENTS:

Introduction

What if positions of power attract psychopathic personalities?
What if we are ruled by psychopaths?
What if our rulers are Satan's Children?

Welcome to Anywhere

'...after Generations Of Struggle against Social Injustice and two Catastrophic And Immensely Bloody Wars with the nearby land of Anotherplace, in which the Ordinary Folk had died and suffered to a catastrophic degree, it was decided by all except the Rapaciously Rich that Things Had To Change.

From that point on, Ordinary Folk were given access to Free Education, Free Healthcare, Pensions, Benefits to help those who fell upon Hard Times and all the advantages of what you would know in your world as a Welfare System. New taxes were introduced to redistribute some of the vast sums of money accumulated (mostly from Stealing, Cheating and Aggressive Tax Avoidance) by the Wealthy and the Aristocracy (known in the land of Anywhere as The Greedy One Percent) over the years and Political Reforms introduced to break their stranglehold over the Political And Economic Life of the country. Additionally, the Right to Vote was given to all.

And the land of Anywhere blossomed, for it was found that a populace Free From Hunger And Illness, that was properly Educated and Cared For, produced huge numbers of Talented men and women who previously had Languished due to Poverty And Lack of Opportunity. These Talented men and women drove the land of Anywhere to new heights of success, founding businesses, employing people, making a mark in the worlds of politics, science, medicine and culture. Slowly but surely, the Dead Grip of The Greedy One Percent, who had dominated and controlled the land of Anywhere for as long as anyone could remember, was broken.'

And the psychopathic Greedy One Percent, Satan's Children, hated this new world, this New Bargain and Better Society, and all it stood for. They vowed to destroy it.

24 Hours

Once upon a time...many, many years ago...*woah! Hold on! Let's just drop the transparent 'Anywhere as Planet Earth' metaphor and set this tale exactly where it actually takes place – your own world, right here and right now...*

One particular day, some time around now, if you like, God (by chance rather design) looked down upon the Earth. This was something He, in his Infinite Wisdom, rarely did. You see, God, by nature, is a tinkerer with a very short attention span and, having created Earth some eons past he had moved on to other things – new planets, new challenges. The fact that Earth was also a failed experiment (that whole Humans and 'free will' thing...well, what a disaster...less said, soonest mended!) that had been at the heart of the rupture between God and his beloved old friend, The Devil, meant that God was even less likely to bother with Earth than any of the other myriad planets he'd created.

But...seeing as planet Earth had come into his view, God decided, reluctantly, that he'd better have a quick look at what was going on, take some notes and do some Supreme Being 'making judgements' type stuff as per the Universe had empowered and mandated him to do.

And so God looked at Earth. And he wished he hadn't.

In England, a prominent politician and a famous celebrity, in a large and richly furnished room in an extremely expensive London property, rape a twelve year old girl. After they've raped her, they murder her...they do this because they enjoy it and because they can get away with it.

In America, a homeless man settles down to try and sleep behind a dumpster, situated down a dank and dark, piss-reeking

New York alleyway; four bankers — drunk on expensive champagne and their own arrogance, have followed him to his insecure, uncomfortable place of rest. They are playing 'hunt the bum'. With laughs and whoops, they kick and stamp the homeless man to death.

In Yemen, 29 school children are blown to pieces by a bomb dropped from a fighter jet flying high above...the children are, apparently, a legitimate military target.

In Brazil, a death squad, sent by a newly elected fascist government (elected with the help and support of Wall Street bankers), kidnaps and murders 12 student activists.

In Spain, a drunken, inadequate man beats his wife to death because she's annoyed him (she's such a nag..) and because she's his property, after all.

In Libya, once a rich nation but destroyed by the greed, avarice and evil of wicked and wealthy old men who dream only of profit and power (you know, the ones who own our politicians...read the next tale), a slave market is trading; women and children fetch the best price — they'll make good money for their new owners as prostitutes and as the unwitting stars of snuff movies; healthy young men are also prized, they'll be killed and their organs harvested and sold to those who are old and sick but wealthy and amoral.

In Nigeria, a two year old child is dying slowly and horribly of starvation whilst, at the same time, a wealthy woman and her husband enters an upmarket store in a fashionable Paris street. She spends $250,000 on a new handbag and he even more on a new watch.

On and on and on it goes, minute after minute, hour after hour...a depressing, sickening litany of murder and evil and injustice and cruelty and tragedy and sadness and prejudice and torture and rape and degradation and stupidity and violence and ignorance.

And God, repulsed and disgusted by all he had seen, thought to himself...

'Oh...what have I done? The Devil was always my Wiser Half...had I but listened to his advice instead of casting him out then I would never even have made this Earth and these horrible humans with their dangerous free will! Maybe now is the time to admit that this Earth and these Humans are, indeed, a failed experiment, a planet and a species inhabited by boundless evil that should be destroyed.'

But then, one hundred miles off the coast of south eastern Spain, a small boat, dangerously overloaded with desperate refugees, men, women and children, fleeing yet another land destroyed and broken by a war fought for no other reason than to make obscene and obscenely rich old men even more obscenely rich, capsizes in rough seas. There are fifty one refugees packed into the boat..most of them are sucked down to their deaths beneath the hungry, cold water with the sinking vessel. Ten minutes later only five people remain alive, bobbing up and down on sharp, serrated waves. Twenty minutes later only three people remain alive, five minutes after that, only two; a young mother and her six month old baby boy.

As she cradles the child in her arms, Nimah (let's dignify this poor young woman with a name for we are, after all, to bare witness to her death) tries pointlessly to shield her infant son from the cold and hostile sea (the boy's name is, was, Malik – what would he have been, what would he have done had he been allowed to grow up rather than been sacrificed for the benefit of the already bulging wallets of the psychopathic elite who rules us?).

The child cries. He's desperately cold and instinctively feels his mothers fear.

Nimah tries hard, so very, very hard, to keep herself and her child afloat, in the hope that help may come. But at some point, Nimah realises that hope of rescue is in vain and she's so tired and so cold...as hope slides away so does her strength....slowly she slips beneath the sea and her last act on this Earth is to put every last ounce of energy she has into lifting Malik up above her head to delay his descent into the cold and hungry ocean; to give him as many last few seconds of this precious gift of life that she possibly can. Finally, as Malik's little head is also embraced by the sea, Nimah summons from somewhere (I would say 'God knows where' but God doesn't actually know half as much as he thinks he does...) the strength to pull the child towards her, to embrace him in her arms and hold him close to her chest. Together they sink down and down, still entwined together in beautiful, selfless, precious love as as their souls leave this Earth, journeying across a Broad, Bright, Blue Sky to That Which Lies Beyond.

So it is that God, seeing this one act of beauty, love, compassion and courage, decides that, no, Planet Earth and it's humans shall not be destroyed! There is still hope! My experiment is not a failure! (If I were to play Devil's Advocate I might say that God seized upon the example of Nimah and her baby boy as an excuse not to face up to his responsibilities, but, well...oh, just read on...you'll get my point).

And, far, far away, the Devil, warmly ensconced in his fiery fortress, chuckles to himself (for the Devil knows us much, much better than God, for this is his world, after all) and says...

'Oh my dear, sweet God, you silly, silly, arrogant old fool, you've fallen for their tricks again haven't you...when will you ever learn to admit your mistakes?'

The New Crown Virus

Once upon a time...in the land of Anywhere, in a world long since forgotten, in the fine and prosperous city of Anyplace there was a secret meeting of a Cabal of psychopaths - that being the Greedy One Percent, the people who really ruled Anywhere, and their minions.

Attending the secret meeting were three extremely wealthy and corrupt individuals (there to represent The Greedy One Percent), members of the Means of Communication (owned by The Greedy One Percent), members of the Swamp State intelligence services (always operating in the service of The Greedy One Percent) and the Leader of the Country (an ignorant, dysfunctional pig of a man who was entirely owned, like all his kind, by The Greedy One Percent)....and, of course, representatives of the Criminal Money Laundering Syndicate, otherwise known as Bankers, were also in attendance (for wherever evil is afoot, you can always find a Banker).

There was a rather difficult issue to discuss. For it was obvious to all that the economy of Anywhere was about to crash very, very badly. This was as a result of it's dependence not on real businesses making real things, but on making money simply by moving money around and investing in complex and deadly financial instruments such as HORFIOD's (Horribly Opaque Risky Financial Instruments Of Death).

The issue was this. Anywhere's economy had already crashed badly (for the reasons described above) some years before. But all had turned out well. The psychopathic elite, knowing the crash was coming, had sold assets at the top of the market and then bought them back (and more) at the bottom of the market, making huge amounts of money in the process. The criminal Bankers, who'd caused the crisis with their fraudulent activities in the first place were 'bailed out' by the government of Anywhere and the whole debacle was paid for by the Ordinary Folk of Anywhere via lower wages, higher taxes, more job insecurity and Austerity. Perfect. As it should be. What's not to like!

So, whilst rather pleased at the idea of a rinse and repeat, boom-bust cycle (mmm, so much money to be made!) Anywhere's psychopathic elite were also a bit nervous that, this crash coming so soon after the last, the Ordinary Folk might, in the common parlance, 'smell a rat': they might lay the blame for the economic crash where it belonged – at the feet of the oligarchs, the criminal Banksters, the Puppet Politicians, the Means of Communication and predatory capitalism and worldization and Austerity. And then, well, they might rise up and demand change...good grief, can you imagine such a thing? How appalling!

How then to have the inevitable and desired crash but not get the blame for it?

Fortunately the Swamp State had the answer. For this meeting of the Cabal of psychopaths had also been called for another reason. Just a few weeks earlier, a new Virus had appeared in the community...from where exactly it was unclear; perhaps it come from bats or birds, cats or chickens or perhaps it had even crossed the Troll/Human barrier...who knew?

A new virus released into the community would be a crisis, yes? Well...yes...but when you're one of The Greedy One Percent a crisis is not so much a crisis as...well...an opportunity.

And this opportunity was explained to the rest of the Cabal by one of the Swamp State creatures.

First, the Means of Communication would move into 24/7 propaganda mode, repeating again and again how widespread the virus was, how deadly it was, how everyone was going to get it, how millions of people would die and (very important) how much the virus would damage the economy and change the world forever. The truth is that the virus was no more or less deadly than a normal annual flu (indeed, it may even have been the normal flu virus rebranded, though it's not for me to speculate..)...but let's not let facts get in the way of a good, economy-crashing, life-destroying panic!

Second, let the Greedy One Percent strike...selling assets as quickly as possible to crash Financial Markets and hurry along the crash.

Third, wait for fear and panic to paralyse commerce and disrupt fragile worldized supply chains and for recession to set in...that'd would also be good for killing thousands and thousands of Ordinary Folk from despair and poverty and hunger..and...of course...all those who died would be classified as dying 'with' The Virus. Fantastic!

Fourth, Puppet Politicians (ably backed by the propaganda peddlers, sorry, Means of Communication) to call for massive financial bail-outs to save the 'economy' because if the 'economy' is not saved there will be no food in the shops, your first-born will have to be sacrificed and the sun will not rise in the morning. The 'economy' is, of course, the banks and large corporations and The Greedy One Percent themselves...it's important to stress that point as one wouldn't want the Ordinary Folk thinking that perhaps all those bail-out funds should actually be used to help them pay their bills, keep a roof over their heads or (can you believe this!) fund proper healthcare services for all!

Five, enjoy the fun! Watch The Ordinary Folk suffer! Watch them die as Healthcare Services are suspended because 'hospitals are over run' and the old, poor and sick die of neglect (sorry, 'with' the virus), then...wow!...just think of the savings in healthcare, pensions and benefits!

Six, introduce lots of anti-democratic laws to restrict freedom of movement, association and expression and close schools and universities (after all, we don't really want the Ordinary Folk to be educated, do we?) to 'slow the spread of the virus' and 'flatten the curve' - none of these thing to be restored after The Virus has gone/served its purpose, obviously.

Seven, after the economy has completely crashed The Greedy One Percent and Banksters to buy back the assets they sold at a high price at a much lower price (plus lots of other cheap goodies!), using their free government supplied bail-out money and The Ordinary Folk will pay for it all through...you guessed it, even lower wages, even more insecure jobs, more unemployment, more taxes and more austerity. But, hey, guys, it wasn't anything to do with us – it was The Virus what did it!

But...there's more! And this is the best bit...Big Drug will make a protection against the virus (and a mountain of money!), let's call it The Medicine, and the Ordinary Folk will have to take The Medicine – and if they don't take The Medicine then they won't get a Medicine Pass and without The Medicine Pass they won't be able to work, shop or even leave the house. And....this just gets better!...eventually The Medicine Pass won't just include information about the last time someone took The Medicine (for The Science will say

The Medicine has to be taken every three months) but also information about a person's friends, associates, what they say on Unsocial Media, what they buy, where they go, their credit history, bank account details...and if there's anything undesirable there, well, that person's Medicine Pass can be switched off and they are locked out of society...not even able to access their own bank account! Fantastic, total control – the Ordinary Folk are now nothing but serfs, owned lock, stock and barrel by The Greedy One Percent!

"They shall own nothing and we will be happy"!

Now at this point, dear reader, you would expect that even a Cabal of Greedy One Percent psychopaths would baulk at such an evil, manipulative and murderous plan? Right? Sorry, you're wrong – they loved the idea, gave the wicked scheme the go ahead and broke into a rousing chorus of their theme tune – 'Cash From Chaos'!

We (oops, sorry, 'the land of Anywhere') truly are ruled by psychopaths...

He Killed The Last Unicorn!

Once upon a time...in the land of Anywhere, in a world long since forgotten, in the fine and prosperous city of Anyplace there lived a Banker. Despite being a rich and seemingly successful individual he was neither particularly bright nor talented – like all his kind he owed his wealth and position to The Magick Of The Old School Tie, a thuggish, brutish (even psychopathic) nature and the easy gains to be made once one was plugged into a Financialised Economic System that owned The Politicians and The Means Of Communication and was blatantly criminal in its nature; that kept all profits to itself but ensured that The Ordinary Folk compensated it for its losses.

In truth, The Banker was a thoroughly unpleasant sort. One of the things he enjoyed doing most, besides Rigging Financial Markets to enrich himself and destroy the lives of others, was hunting. He loved to dress himself up in the latest style of Aristocratic Idiot hunting gear and stroll pompously through the wild countryside surrounding the city of Anyplace, various guides, scouts and gillies In Attendance, killing as many animals as possible. For no other reason than entertainment and the satisfaction of his gross appetites. Oh, and to validate himself as a man for he was, in reality, so inadequate as one that only killing things made him feel like a Proper Person.

One day, on one of those hunts The Banker enjoyed so much, he wondered somewhat Off The Beaten Track, away from those In Attendance, and found himself alone, forcing his way through an area of low, dense scrub and towering trees. He found that being alone actually made him feel More Of A Man and his excitement at the prospect of killing some poor animal became even more intense. That excitement grew markedly when he found himself in a clearing amongst the trees and scrub and saw, just ahead, unaware of his presence, chewing on a clump of lush grass – a Unicorn! The beautiful, extraordinary, almost mythical Unicorn. The ultimate hunter's trophy!

And therein lays our tale. For this Unicorn, chewing away peacefully on a clump of God's Green Grass in front of our vile Banker, was The Last Unicorn. The only one left in existence after widespread depredation and pollution of the Natural Environment by The Greedy One Percent and constant hunting by them and their Minions. To kill this one, fine and beautiful animal would permanently unstitch one of the Threads Of Creation from the Cloth Of The Universe. If The Banker had known this, would it have made any difference to his intention and desire to kill the animal? No, indeed it would have made the kill all the sweeter. Would it have made any difference to him if he had known that the act of removing A Thing Of Beauty forever from the fabric of the Universe would curse his Soul? No, for he would have thought that but a small problem that could be dealt with as any problem is dealt with – with money.

Oblivious of all the matters we have just discussed (for he was oblivious to all except money, power and self-gratification), The Banker raised his rifle to his shoulder and placed the Unicorn in his sights. But just as he was about to pull back the trigger and let fly a slug of hot, fatal metal - up popped a Faerie! As Faeries are wont to do in such circumstance s.

Don't ask me where the Faerie had been, or where she had come from. I've no idea. Nobody knows how Faeries materialise and dematerialise at crucial and significant times, except perhaps because they are drawn to strong emotion like bees to honey – beyond that, it's impossible to explain, simply part of Faerie Magick, beyond the experience or knowledge of men. What I can say for sure is that the Faerie had materialised at this point and space in time to prevent a Gross Crime Against The Universe. It had determined that the last Unicorn was in danger of being killed and had decided it had to try to stop this awful event from occurring.

To this end, the Faerie materialised, with a pop and a bang, directly in front of the barrel of The Banker's gun. Flapping her diaphanous but powerful little wings she held a tiny hand, palm facing forward, to The Banker and said, 'stop, you cannot kill this Unicorn – it is the last of its kind and its death would be a Grievous Affront to the Universe!'

Now at this point, The Banker showed himself to be truly an ignorant man who knew everything of the ways of the world but nothing about the way the world worked. He should have realised that you never mess with a Faerie and if they tell you directly to something, you do it. He should have said, 'yes, Faerie' and 'of course, Faerie', instead he said:

'Hah, get out the way, Faerie, who are you to tell me what to do? This animal is mine, I shall have its head on my wall!'

'Do you not understand,' replied the Faerie, somewhat puzzled by this man's stupidity, 'this is the *last* Unicorn – if you remove a thing of such beauty from the Universe your Soul will be damned?'

'Oh shut up, Faerie, with your stupid talk of Souls and damnation...this is no longer your world and your so-called Magick has no power, your time has passed - the power of the age is money for money overcomes anything and I am a Man Of Money so your mumblings mean nothing to me!'

'Look,' said the Faerie, trying one more time to do the best for all concerned, 'it seems to me that Man Of Money you may be but man of sense, knowledge and wisdom you most definitely are not...do not do this, the consequences of your actions will be dire! I cannot stop you doing it, only try and persuade you, for I have to respect the Universal Law of Free Will, but if you do it do it, I warn you...I will bite you!'

At this point any sensible person would have turned heel and run, for to be bitten by a Faerie is to be cursed by a Faerie. Faerie Bites never, ever end well. But instead The Banker laughed, 'ha, ha...is that it? Is that the sum total of your pathetic power...you'll bite me! Why you are tiny and such a bite would be no more consequential than a gnat bit to me!'

'Anyway...you said it yourself, you cannot stop me...'

'But I beg you...please don't...'

'You cannot stop me, can you, Faerie?'

'No, regretfully, no...'

'Well then!'

And with that The Banker shoved the Faerie violently out of the way with the barrel of his gun and pulled the trigger. Gas exploded and expanded hugely and rapidly behind cold, hard metal and a super-charged slug of death sped through the air, taking the life of the Unicorn but milliseconds later. And a creature of such grace and beauty that it would become a thing of myth in not just one but many worlds, was Taken From Existence forever and we all became the poorer for it.

Seeing the Unicorn fall dead to the ground, The Banker jumped up and down, ecstatic, waving his gun above his head – not remotely upset that he had just removed a Thing Of Beauty from the Fabric of the Universe forever, just delighted that he'd killed something –even better, something so rare, the last of its kind, even!

The Faerie meanwhile observed events with despair and as the Unicorn died she shed a single Faerie tear of sadness, which turned into a diamond as it rolled down her cheek (as Faerie tears do) and dropped to the ground, its Shining Beauty lost forever in the dirt. But her job here was not yet done. In the blink of an eye she flew at The Banker, planting a Faerie bite in the middle of his forehead, just below his hairline. And then off she went - dematerialising and popping up at another intersection of time and space, deeply regretful that she had failed in her attempt to save the Unicorn but confident that the correct punishment had been meted out for such a heinous act.

The Banker was aware of none of this, he feared no Faerie and he feared no punishment, he was too rich to be punished after all! Attracted by his cries of jubilation, those In Attendance soon found him. He instructed them to take the Unicorn's head and have it stuffed and mounted. So happy was he that he decided to forgo returning to his wife and children in his palatial mansion in the hills outside of Anyplace, instead he would go to his townhouse in the city and treat himself to a whore to celebrate his fabulously successful hunt!

He was vaguely aware of a slight itching and a smudge of blood in the centre of his forehead, just below the hairline but gave it no import. It was surely nothing more than a Silly Little Gnat Bite.

The Banker proceeded with his plans. He went to his townhouse (in one of the most elegant and upmarket districts of Anyplace) and had the whore he'd promised himself. After the sex act had taken place, rather than pay the woman for services rendered, he beat her up and threw her out into the street. The Banker, and his kind, cannot approach any transaction fairly; they always, always have to make on Both Ends Of The Deal.

Later that night The Banker was lying asleep in his big, comfortable bed in his big comfortable house. He was dreaming happily about money and killing things. Were there any more species on the edge of extinction that he could kill? Suddenly he was awoken from his pleasant dream musings by an irritating itch in the centre of his forehead, just below the hairline. Humph, that damn gnat bite! he thought. He was also aware that he was feeling nauseous and feverish, in fact he was sweating buckets; he put a hand up to his forehead to examine the source of the annoying itching to find that what had been a tiny bite had swelled to the size of an egg! What was this? What was going on?

The Banker decided that he should get up out of bed, look at this strange growth in the mirror...

'Your soul will be damned...'

'I'll bite you...'

The Faeire's words ran around a dimly lit, rarely used corner of his mind and rose up into his consciousness, a little bubble of terror popping open – sudden realisation that a Faerie Bite was a Faerie Curse. Damn, perhaps he should have listened to the annoying Faerie...not killed the Unicorn...but, no, no, the thing on his forehead was but a bump. Maybe a septic gnat bite, nothing more, he was a man of Money, a man of Power, he had nothing to fear either from a bite gone bad or stupid Faeries spouting arcane nonsense about bites, curses and damnation! Hah! This is the Modern World, a world of Money not Magick!

Reassured, by his sensible, logical thoughts The Banker made to get up from his bed, have a look at the strange bump on his forehead and put some antiseptic on it. But he found he couldn't. He simply couldn't persuade his body to move. For not only was he feverish and nauseous he also weak, incredibly weak, his body simply wouldn't do what his mind wanted it to do. The irritation from the thing on his forehead reached a new pitch – what had just been itching was now a dull, painful throbbing. With effort, for he seemed to be getting weaker with every passing second, he lifted hand to forehead and examined the bump again. It was now even bigger! Warm. Throbbing. Painful. Malicious. Vengeful. Just under the surface of the bump he could feel something very hard, very pointed. Now the bump became the source of not just pain but excruciating, eye-crossing pain. And it exploded open in a shower of blood that The Banker could feel and see splattering across the ceiling above him and settling down as a fine, red mist across his face and his big, comfortable bed. Something was growing out of the centre of his forehead, just below the hairline. Something hard, pointed with a curled pattern running from top to bottom, wider at the base than at the sharp, pointed tip.

Oh, no...

Please no...

Oh God, please, not that....

What was growing from The Banker's forehead was a horn. A Unicorn Horn. And even as The Banker touched the horn, it grew and grew and the Pain Of Growth was like a nail being hammered into his brain. He screamed and screamed in utter agony. He tried once more to move, to get out his bed and run, somewhere, anywhere; but his body now had even less strength than just minutes ago...his hand slumped away from the thing growing out of him and lay inert and useless on a fine, goose feather pillow. Now he could move only his eyes. He rolled them back, upwards and the horn growing up from his forehead came into his field of vision. And The Bankers worst fears were confirmed, it was undoubtedly and unmistakably a Unicorn's Horn.

The pain stopped. The horn ceased its growth and The Banker ceased his screams. Silence reigned. The Silence Of The Grave.

That silence lasted only seconds. Because The Banker heard a strange collection of noises. Breathing, something that resembled a heavy foot stamping on the floor and...neighing.

Like a horse.

Like a...Unicorn.

The Banker rolled his eyes towards the source of the strange noises and his heart filled with terror...for there, in his room, was the Unicorn he had Taken From The Universe. And The Unicorn was staring at The Banker with a look of sheer, pure, unadulterated, vengeful hatred.

The Banker's pitiful, terrified screaming began again, and The Unicorn began to glow with a cold, unearthly blue light, a glow taken up by the horn sprouting from The Bankers forehead. And as well as glowing, the horn started to grow faster - and bigger. It grew and grew until it reached the ceiling of The Bankers bedroom, at which point it attained some kind of Magickal Flexibilty. It whirled around and around above The Banker and then struck down with great speed and force, plunging its sharp point deep into his genitals with a crunching sound and a huge gout of blood. The Banker's screams reached a new intensity. The horn withdrew itself, tip covered in blood and torn flesh, from The Bankers genital area and reared up and back and, in a move as gentle and careful and precise as the previous one had been swift and brutal, it popped first one of his eyeballs and then the other.

The helpless, dying banker screamed and screamed and screamed and begged for a Mercy That Was Not Forthcoming. The horn reared and plunged again and again, now with great violence, peppering The Banker's body with horrific wounds until he died and his rotten Soul exited his body to slink down to Hell and that Special Place that The Devil keeps for his Special Children.

All this was watched by The Unicorn who now wore on his face, if a Unicorn can wear such, a look of Great Satisfaction. The Unicorn observed events until The Banker's life expired and returned to wherever it had been Magicked from. With The Unicorn's departure, the horn atop The Banker's head lost the ghostly life that had entered it, shrank back and stilled and solidified. But it was still a fine Unicorn Horn protruding from a Banker's head.

The Banker's body was not discovered for several days. No neighbours had heard his dying screams and alerted the authorities for the neighbouring properties (like most of the properties in that area of Anyplace) were empty, having been bought not to live in but for Investment Purposes by members of The Greedy One Percent looking for ways to launder their ill-gotten gains. Nor was anyone (including wife and children) in a hurry to report The Bankers absence from place of work or marital home. People feared the man, but did not like nor respect him; his absence was a source of relief, not concern.

When The Bankers horribly mutilated, rotting corpse was finally discovered no coherent explanation could be found for the large Unicorn Horn growing from the middle of his forehead, just below the hairline. The cause of death would be listed as 'Death By Magick'.

And the moral of this tale is: 'there really are more things in heaven and earth...than are dreamt of in your philosophy.' (With thanks to Mr. Shakespeare).

Why Trolls Hate Bankers

Once upon a time... many, many years ago in a world long since forgotten, there was a country called Anywhere. And in the land of Anywhere there was a fine and prosperous city called Anyplace and one day, many miles away from this illustrious city, across mountain and moor, valley and peak, a lone Troll was searching for rurt mushrooms.

Now rurt mushrooms are a Great Delicacy in the Troll world. They are rare and hard to find as they grow only in the most inhospitable and isolated parts of Anywhere but Trolls, such is their love for rurts, will travel long distances to harvest them.

Our particular Troll, then, was about a day's journey away from his Troll hole (and that at the incredible speed that a Troll In A Hurry can attain). As the Troll Squidged And Squodged through boggy ground, he was lashed by a Cold Rain and a Strong Wind. But he minded none of this; he was a Happy Troll for already he had gathered many rurts and had stashed them safely away in the large sack he had brought with him. He couldn't wait to see the smiles on the faces of his Troll Wife and twin boy Trollettes when he showed them his fine harvest! It was for them he was a gathering rurts: they were to be the centrepiece of a fine Birthday Feast for his beloved Trolletes, who very soon would celebrate their tenth birthday.

When the Troll's sack was Full To Bursting, he finally decided he had enough of the delicious mushrooms and began his homeward journey. He ran as fast as his powerful Troll legs could carry him, he ran through rain and wind, through light and darkness, full of excitement for the Birthday Feast to come.

But the Troll's homecoming was not to be a happy one, for he was to discover that in his absence, the Blind Old Weaver Of Fate had spun some threads that were Exceptionally Cruel even by her own Maliciously Random standards.

The first sign something was Not Quite Right came as the Troll approached his Troll hole. He could see it in the near distance, but no smoke was rising from the chimney of his comfortable home. And on a cold day like this? How strange. And as the Troll approached nearer his home things grew stranger for he became aware of an Absence Of Noise. The Trollettes were boisterous things and constantly on the go, banging and smashing their way through their young lives. Why so quiet?

At this point a Cold Spot opened up somewhere deep inside the Troll. Panicked, he ran even faster than is usual for a Troll, eager to eat up the remaining space between him and his Troll hole. He knew, just knew, that Something Was Very, Very Wrong.

Faster than you can say "Blimey, Trolls are big aren't they," the Troll was at the door of his Troll hole. He pushed it open and Despair overwhelmed him like a Huge Black Wave. For all was quite, yet all was chaos. Inside his home furniture had been Upended And Upturned, personal effects and clothing were strewn all around, blood was spattered on the walls and pooling on the floor; there was the Scent Of Death. The Troll stared in wide-eyed Horror And Disbelief. There, in front of him, on the floor of his once comfortable home, not two arm's length, but a Universe and Another Life away, lay the battered and mutilated bodies of his beloved Troll wife and and his two darling Trollettes.

The Troll collapsed to his knees, hands thrown up to his face, and let out a howl of rage and despair and of unbridgeable, unfathomable loss. That howl was so loud that it shook the very ground and was heard by every Troll within a hundred mile radius who, upon hearing it, paused a minute in what they were doing and shed a tear of Sympathy And Love for the Deep, Abiding Loss of a Friend They Had Not Yet Met. The Troll fled his ruined home and ran outside, collapsing to the ground, rolling and pulling out his fur with his strong hands in great clumps. The fine fur caught the wind and floated up and away, just as the Souls of his wife and Trollettes had already done.

As our unhappy Troll lay there crying, shaking, sobbing and occasionally screaming, a Faerie (attracted by strong emotions like a Bee To Honey, as Faeries are) popped up. She hovered over the Troll and looked down at him and she felt great pity for she could almost taste his Despair And Loss. Looking into his Soul she saw all that happened to him, and all that could happen to him, all that he was and all that he could be. And she shuddered inwardly as she Looked Further Afield and saw what had happened to the Troll's wife and Trollettes.

In her wisdom, the Faerie saw that the Universe Required that she Reach Out to and help this Sad And Broken Troll. "Troll, poor, poor Troll," she said, "I am so sorry, let me hug you and share your grief."

Now given the Vast Disparity in size between a Troll and a Faerie, a Faerie giving a Troll a hug is a physical impossibility but the Faerie had an answer for that. She went one better than a hug; she reached out two big, strong Spiritual Arms that enfolded the Troll in Warm Comfort, holding him tight, stroking the back of his furry head and soothing his Soul.

Eventually the Troll's agitation calmed somewhat, but still the Faerie held him: two creatures come together as one in the Infinite Vastness Of Time, in the midst of a large empty landscape, in a land long forgotten, in another world: such is the Curious Randomness of the Universe.

And then the Troll did a very wise thing. Now fully composed and full of a grim and cold determination, he asked the Faerie a question. Your own world lacking in Magick you will not know this, but one of the many Peculiarities of Faeries is that if you should meet one and ask her a Direct Question she is bound to give you a Truthful Answer. Beware though, this particular rule (which, strangely, would also apply if you were unfortunate enough to meet The Devil) applies only to your first question. After that its pot luck I'm afraid, as is much with any Faerie related dealings you may have.

The question the Troll answered was this: "Faerie, tell me truthfully, as you are bound to do, who killed my family?"

Our little Faerie paused. She was fully aware she had to give an Honest Answer, but feared she may be about to open a Pandora's Box. But...a Universal Directive is a Universal Directive, so she answered..."humans, Troll, it was humans, Bankers to be exact. They find amusement in hunting and murdering Trolls. They are bad people even by human standards, people who have sold their Souls to an evil and entirely abstract concept called money."

"Humans, hah, I should have known," said a Furious looking Troll, "I know nothing of this money thing you talk about, but I know full well of human evil...they have been stealing our land and persecuting us for generations, they are nothing but children of the Devil."

"I grant you, Troll, that humans are a race who seem particularly prone to cruelty. But remember that not all of them are bad , remember that, Troll...they're not all evil. Forget my words and you will become no better than the humans who have so grievously hurt you, this is my warning to you, Troll, for I have seen all that you have been, all that you are and all that you could be."

"Having used your powers to see so much about me, Faerie, you will also know that from here I intend to travel to that hideous hive of humanity, the city they call Anyplace, and kill as many humans as I possibly can. I will have my vengeance, Faerie. I thank you for the kindness you have shown me today but as a Troll my duty is to hold dear the virtues of Good And Decency and when these virtues are threatened and Evil disturbs the Equilibrium Of The Universe then those have sown the Bad Seeds must reap the Bitter Harvest. This is a Universal Truth that even God himself accepts."

"I have no argument with you, my dear Troll. I fully understand your need for vengeance, indeed I applaud it, but I ask you aim it at those who deserve it. Look, I do not wish to see you lose your Soul and become as the evil Bankers who slaughtered your family, so I will give you a Faerie Gift."

"Hold...stay your wand, Faerie. Will this be a gift that is true, or one with mischief hidden in it somewhere?"

The Faerie laughed at this comment from the Troll, for Faerie gifts really are notoriously unpredictable, and replied "no, Troll, no mischief...just a pure gift!"

"In that case, please give me your gift. I thank you for it, Faerie and I thank you again for the deep kindness you have shown me."

"Kindness is everything, my dear Troll, kindness is everything. One final piece of advice, dear Troll, Evil smells foul but the Evil you seek smells foulest."

And with that typically cryptic comment, the Faerie gave the Troll the gift of being able to smell good and evil in people.

After the Faerie left him, the Troll set about the Grim And Tragic Task of burying his wife and Trollettes. As is Troll tradition, he dug a large hole in the ground exactly two hundred Troll paces from his Troll hole and aligned to the direction of the setting sun. Lovingly and with Utmost Care he laid the bodies of his Precious Ones in the freshly dug grave. He also placed in the grave the collection of Faerie diamonds, those that had been cried by a Faerie at his and his dead wife's Wedding Ceremony. (Every Troll wedding is attended by a Faerie who cries tears of joy when the couple exchange vows, these Diamond Tears are then collected and saved as a precious momento by the couple and, traditionally, buried with first partner who passes away). He also wanted to bury the Trollettes favourite Teddy Troll with their Precious Little Bodies (a big orange and yellow stuffed toy in the shape of Old Father Troll that he'd won for them in an arm-wrestling contest at last year's Annual Troll Fair) but was, strangely, unable to find it. Instead he made do with the first pairs of shoes the Trollettes had ever worn, beautifully crafted, tiny little things, made of the softest of leather and charmingly embroided with Snow Trolls made of silken thread.

And with that, all was ready. Before filling the grave with Earth, observing one final Troll tradition, the Troll took a knife and cut off the little finger of his left hand and dropped it into the grave, to rest there with his family until that time when, somewhere along the Infinite Circle that is life, death and rebirth, their Souls would all, once again, be reunited.

Two days later, after a long and arduous journey in which he was again and again haunted by images of his wife and Trollettes, the Troll finally arrived at the city of Anywhere. Thanks to the remarkable and entirely instinctive sense of time, speed and distance that Trolls possess he arrived, Exactly As Planned, late at night and, Under Cover Of Darkness and by using his remarkable Speed And Stealth was soon deep within the city.

However... it being late at night, and a cold and miserable winter's night at that, the Troll found his Burning Desire for revenge Somewhat Thwarted. For there were no humans to be seen, not a one. For an hour or more the Troll wandered empty streets, amazed and unsettled by the closely packed buildings of the city and the cold, dead weight of stone and metal that it was made up of. He was beginning to think his plan for vengeance would Come To Naught, that he simply wouldn't find any humans to kill and he cried tears of bitter frustration at the thought of his loved ones' murder going unavenged. But then, finally, turning into the street ahead of him, he saw a human. From hair and shape he judged it to be a female: female humans he knew, as all Trolls do, are generally (though not, it must be said, always) less evil than male ones. Still, she was a human, she would be the first to die. Now, whilst the Troll could see that this human was a lady, what he could not see (for he was Troll not Faerie, after all) was that this lady was a Good Person. She was the only human out that night in that part of the city as she was on her way to work the night shift as a cleaner at The Asylum For The Strange And The Different, that being just one of three jobs she worked to help support her family. She was a lovely lady. Had you known her in your world you would have liked her: a kind lady, full of Goodness And Grace. She did not deserve to die and her death, as had warned the Faerie, would cost the Troll his Soul.

Tip-toeing quietly and stealthily on the very end of his very, very big toes, the Troll approached the lady from behind, dark clouds of vengeance filling his mind.

And then he abruptly stopped.

For just feet in front of him the lady had pulled to a sharp halt, with one foot poised hanging in the air. For the lady, in the dim glow cast by a street lamp, had seen a snail on the pavement beneath, her foot being about to crush that very same snail, she had halted its downward movement. Her head full of strange thoughts and images of the Blind Old Weaver Of Fate, randomly spinning Malicious Threads Of Misfortune into the cloth of someone's life and ruining that person's life forever, she determined that she would not do the same. She would not crush the life out of this small, defenceless snail in the same random, unthinking way that the Blind Old Weaver crushed Life And Hope out of so many. She let down her dangling foot to the side of the snail, bent down, picked it up, placed it on a nearby wall where it would be safe from crushing and could live its life at its own slow, snail pace and its tiny, Unblemished snail Soul make its final journey across a Broad,

Bright, Blue Sky when it was good and ready to do so and not before.

Just as the lady placed the little snail on the wall, the nostrils of the Silently Observing Troll were filled with the wonderful scent of freshly baked brucht (brucht being the Troll equivalent of what you call in your world bread) and in a moment the Troll understood. It was the Faerie Gift. He could smell Good and Evil and, of course, Good smelt wonderful. Just like the smell of freshly baked brucht that the Troll now knew was emanating from the lady in front of him. This human female was obviously a Good person. To kill her would serve no purpose. Indeed it would upset the Equilibrium Of The Universe, it would be a repayment of an Evil with another Evil act, an action that would lose the Troll his soul.

Leaving the Good Lady be, the Troll slunk back into the shadows, thanking the Troll Father for the Faerie's spell. He now knew what he needed to do. He needed to locate the Bankers who had taken everything from him and kill them and only them. And he knew exactly how to do it. If the Faerie spell had allowed him to smell the Good in the Lady, then if he concentrated hard enough if he'd be able to smell the Evil of the murdering Bankers. And so the Troll concentrated. He inhaled deeply and his senses were assaulted by a wave of foul smelling corruption, for this was a human city and was awash with evil. But the Troll had remembered the Faeries words - that the Evil he sought smelt the foulest - so, with great effort he sought out the worst smelling scent amongst the wave of smell that surrounded him...and found it! There! That thread of rotting meat, of putrid dung. That's them. The Bankers. Time to do some killing!

So, the Troll followed his, nose. All the way, out of the city, to the hills just outside, where the stood the Opulent Mansions of the fabulously wealthy Greedy One Percent. And as the sun rose, he tracked it to its very epicentre, a particularly large mansion, surrounded by a wall that was the height of two men. This was it. Whoever lived here had killed his family. With one great Troll jump the Troll was over the wall and into the gardens of the mansion, speeding up to the house itself. The Scent Of Evil led the Troll round to the back of house, and from a nearby set of large glass doors he could hear voices. Quietly he approached. Through the doors he could see four people gathered round a table, a woman, a smartly dressed man and two younger humans, also smartly dressed. In fact, the Troll was seeing a family, but not like his own. The woman was the wife, the smartly dressed man the father and the two younger humans the sons. The father was, indeed, a Banker, a very High-Up and Prominent One. The sons were both in their early twenties and had their own mansions nearby and they (such is Magick Of The Old School Tie) worked in the same bank as their father. It was a tradition for them to meet for breakfast at the father's mansion before they all travelled to work together for another day of Corrupt Dealings and Financial Manipulation at the Bank.

As the Troll stood there, On The Outside Looking In, one of the sons suddenly pointed at something lying, bloodstained and forlorn, in the middle of the table around which the humans were sat and all three of the male laughed. The Troll's eyes followed the pointing finger and he was filled with Overwhelming Rage. For what he saw was his Trollettes' Teddy Troll. In a Thunderous Explosion of a Million Crystals he burst through the glass doors into the Banker's home and yelled at the occupants to stay still. Very still. Or die. Which one was it? Which one of these people had killed his family? As the humans sat drop-jawed and petrified (if you've ever had a Troll smash his way into your kitchen early in the morning then you would understand their reaction, trust me) the Troll inhaled hugely and realised that all three of the male humans were exuding the Scent Of Evil. All three had done it, all three had killed his family...what fun they must have had defiling, torturing and mutilating: and what a price they were going to pay.

The Troll shouted to the woman to leave, to run and not come back, for she smelt only of a Lesser Evil. She didn't need telling again, she was off and away. She'd only married the vile Old Git for his money, she didn't like him and the children she'd spawned by him were just as bad. She had no intention whatsoever of sticking around in the face of an obviously Very Angry Troll.

Upon the hurried departure of the women, the Troll gathered the Shocked Into Stillness bankers up in his huge arms; the father under one arm, the two sons under the other - a small burden for Trolls who are Massively Strong.

Charging at maximum Troll speed out of the house, he ran down a long driveway to the imposing wooden gates of the Opulent Mansion, crashing through them, leaving only splinters behind, and made his way out of the hills that house Enviable Homes of the Greedy One Percent.

The Troll did not stop until he'd reached a dense forest far, far away from Anyplace. Coming to a small clearing in the trees he stopped and threw the humans to the floor. They were crying, bawling, begging to be released, constantly telling the Troll how much money they would give him would he but release them. The Troll paid them No Heed. He ripped off their expensive clothes and used the remains to bind them hand and foot: annoyed by their constant whining, he stuffed their mouths with twigs and leaves.

He then set about digging a hole, a big hole, a deep hole. His powerful arms and shovel-sized hands soon accomplished this task. He stood back from his work, and gave a grunt of satisfaction, for the hole was Fit For Purpose. Turning to face the shivering, crying and absolutely terrified bankers, he addressed them "you humans killed my family, an act of unspeakable evil. You took from me all that mattered to me, you took that which I loved and spat on it and beat it and cut it and mutilated it and destroyed it...and to you, to you...it was something...*funny!* Something you could talk and laugh about over breakfast! But now, now you must pay the price. You three have taken all that is Good And Decent and trod it under foot! As a Troll I am sworn to defend these Blessed Virtues and for this reason, and for my murdered family, it is my duty to remove you from this world for Corrupted creatures like you are a disease that eats all around them..." the Troll paused, seemed to have run out of words. Actually...he *had* run out of words for Trolls are not big talkers so he decided to speed things on to the good bit, the part he was going to enjoy and said, quite abruptly, "I judge you guilty of the crime of murder, the sentence is death!"

And one by one, he gathered the Bankers and hurled them, struggling madly, into the deep hole he had dug. When all three were lying, flopping like fish out of water, at the bottom of the hole, he straddled it with his big Troll legs, squatted and emptied his bowels, releasing a torrent of thick and pungent Troll excrement onto the bankers below.

Then, slowly, very slowly, a handful at a time, he began to refill the hole with earth and carried on doing so until the Bankers were buried alive and their black Souls oozed from their bodies to travel to the Dark Place where the Devil keeps his Special Children.

Foreclosure

Once upon a time... in the land of Anywhere, in a world long since forgotten, in the fine and prosperous city of Anyplace there was a Banker and on the day that our story starts this particular Banker was particularly happy for today was a Foreclosure Day. And he was going to have such fun! For today a desperate lady was due to come and see him to try and plead her case for the Bank to not foreclose on her mortgage, leaving her and her young family homeless.

Now, before we go any further, you need to know that our Banker was not some humble apprentice sociopath Bank Manager, He was a full-on, fully-fledged sociopath; he was a Director of the Bank. There was, in reality, absolutely no reason why he should meet with a 'customer' (as the Bank laughingly referred to its victims) who was due to be foreclosed and evicted, as he had many Minions who could perform such a task. But...the Banker was (see above) a sociopath and a sadist and, truth be told, he just loved having a meeting with some poor and desperate person who was begging for a chance to keep their home so he could smile smugly at them, remind them of their stupidity in not paying their mortgage and refuse to help. So...given that, every time some poor fool who thought that they might be able to change the Bank's Decision, was due to come in for a meeting to discuss such aim, the Banker had instructed his Minions to inform him of the event; he would then, time permitting, hold the meeting himself.

So it was that the Banker found himself sitting in his plush chair in his plush office, delighting in the Pathetic Pleadings of the pathetic Ordinary Person, a meek and mousey young woman, sat before him...

"I know we are three months behind with the mortgage but that is because my husband had an accident and could not work, and then there was the cost of the healthcare...he would be here today but he's better now and working every hour that God sends...I, myself, also work as many hours I can but I have two young children so I cannot work full time..."

"Hah," said the Banker, "there you go then...you would not be in this mess had you just apprenticed the children to The Factory."

"But, sir...they are too young as they are not yet twelve years of age."

"Hah, then you should have put them into nursery for the entire day so you could work more hours!"

"But, sir, child care has to be paid for nowadays and the cost would be more than I could earn in my minimum wage job."

"Hah, then your husband should not have become ill – no doubt that happened because he was feckless and ignorant and ate the wrong kind of food."

"No, sir! We eat as well as we can afford too and my husband illness was a result of exposure to toxic chemicals at his previous work place...this kind of things happens all the time nowadays, ever since the government abolished health and safety regulations...

"Stop! Now you're just trying to justify your own stupidity! Look, let's be honest, you and your husband obviously aren't clever enough to earn a decent wage so you shouldn't have taken on a mortgage in the first place..."

"But, sir. We are both university graduates...we've taken the best jobs we could find...good jobs are few and far between in the modern labour market and those that there are are reserved for the children of the already rich."

"Oh, what nonsense woman, conspiracy theory twaddle!" replied the Banker...really enjoying himself now, for he could see desperation written over the woman's face. "You and your Feckless Family are not the Bank's responsibility, your home shall be ours, you and your mewling brats can pitch a tent somewhere until such time as the Free Market and Trickle Down Economics save you."

"Please, sir, please...think of my children, how will they cope on the street...we're only three months behind...could you not give us a bit more time to pay?"

"No, because you have bad credit." (This is fun now! thought the Banker)

"Could we not extend the period of the mortgage and lower the monthly payments?"

"No, because you have bad credit." (Oh, I'm loving this! thought the Banker).

"Could we not pay the missed payments off a bit every month?"

"No, because you have bad credit." (Look at the sad bitch squirm, hah, hilarious! thought the banker).

"Is there not anything at all that you would consider so that we could save our home?"

"You could try begging me..."

"I'm sorry..." (Mmm, thought the Banker and subtly slipped a hand beneath his desk and rubbed himself down there).

"Maybe if you beg me I'll let you keep your home..."

"Then I beg you, please, it's been such a hard year, I don't think my family would survive being made homeless...oh, my poor children...please, please don't do this..."

"Oh well, now...let me think...should you keep your home...hmm?" (A silence so intense and deep you could hear the proverbial pin drop). "Hmm...NO! Because you still have bad credit...there really is nothing more to be said, your home now belongs to the Bank so I suggest you leave here, pack up your pathetic possessions and horrible children and make alternative arrangements!"

The woman looked at the Banker, face and eyes empty of hope. She stood, unsteadily, turned around and walked away to an Uncertain Future. As she closed the door to the Banker's office he burst into laughter, delighted to hear her crying. What an excellent meeting! An asset recovered for the Bank, an Ordinary Person put in their place and the life of an entire family ruined. A good day's work! The Banker sat back into his comfortable chair and smiled happily to himself, positively tumescent with pleasure!

Had the Banker been aware, at that point, that his entire meeting with the sad, and now homeless, lady had been observed by an unseen third party he would not have been so happy. And if he had known that that observer had been a Faerie, who had 'popped up' (as Faeries do when humans give off strong emotions) in the exact same time and space as the Banker's meeting he would have been even less happy.

And with good reason. For the Faerie had been appalled by the Banker's callous, blustering, arrogant and downright nasty performance. She resolved that some harmony should be put back into The Universe – an unpleasant Banker needed to be punished.

With that in mind, she flew to the wild countryside outside the city of Anyplace to have a word with a Troll who owed her a favour.

Later that day, late at night in fact, the Banker was sleazing his way down a dark back alley in the Downtown area of Anyplace, en route to one of the many brothels this part of Anyplace is famous for, you see – and there's no delicate way to put this so I'll be frank - humiliating the poor woman who had come to see him earlier in the day, mocking her, taking her home off her, rendering her destitute. Well. All that had made him horny as Hell. So, off, to a brothel it was – in fact, the Banker had one particular brothel in mind, an expensive and exclusive one that catered for men of his income, taste and morality – one that had an extensive stock of underage girls, trafficked into Anywhere from the impoverished land of Farawayplace. He was going to sully and bruise some firm, young flesh, yum!

But the Banker never made his so anticipated late night appointment with Rape and Degradation, for half way down that dark back alley he was snatched by a large and powerful Troll who, earlier that day, had had a conversation with a certain Faerie.

Everything happened so quickly that the Banker had no time to react; one minute he was thinking happy thoughts about abusing some poor young girl and the next minute he found himself scooped up under one powerful arm of a huge Troll that was speeding (and a speeding Troll is very fast indeed) its way out of Anyplace, out past the hills that surround the city, into the wild countryside to a steep and isolated mountain range. The Troll/Banker kidnap scenario was witnessed by a few of Anyplace's citizens but, taking to heart the old Anywhere adage 'where there's a Troll involved, don't get involved', they averted their eyes and kept their mouths shut.

By and by, the Troll arrive at his desired destination – a deep and complex cave system high up in the aforementioned mountain range, a place known only to Trolls, a place they keep secret where Acts and Rituals are performed such as humans would not understand and which you, gentle reader, are better off knowing nothing about.

At some point in his kidnap by the Troll the Banker, the air squeezed out of him by the Troll's ridiculously strong grasp and in a state of total panic, had passed out. When he awoke, he found himself in a bare and bleak cell of stone - one which had no windows or visible door and which was lit only by a dimly glowing ball of light hanging from the ceiling, that seemed Magickal in its origin. The Banker could also see that in one corner of the cell was a dimly glowing ball of orange light emitting heat (which seemed equally Magickal in origin). Besides that, the cell contained only a thin mattress of Rough and Mean material and a rickety table upon which was placed some bread (old, dry and, quite frankly, well past its best), a large jug of water and four gold coins.

What witchery is this? thought the Banker, staring at his new surroundings with complete befuddlement, what the?..fragments of memory returned...a dark alley, an expectation of perverse pleasure...then a huge looming shape with lots of fur and big horns...that could only be a Troll!

"Nooooo!" screamed the Banker. "Where am I? Who has done this to me? Speak to me!"

Silence.

"Troll, Troll...I know you are there and I know you are a Troll! Let me go now ,Troll...if you don't I'll make you sorry..."

"Hullo, Banker," came a deep and disembodied voice from somewhere indefinable outside of the Banker's cell, "I am the Troll, the one who took you...tell me, exactly what will you do if I don't free you?"

"Troll," replied the Banker, "I am a man of Power and Wealth, I warn you...there are many ways that one as Rich as I can punish if you do not do my bidding...or even reward you if you do..."

"Hah! How ignorant you and your like are of the Universe, Banker, for all your money and wealth mean nothing here"

"What do you mean? Nonsense, you are obviously holding me here because you hope I'll pay money for my freedom...everyone wants money, money is everything to everyone so stop talking nonsense and just tell me the Price of my Freedom"

"Freedom has no price, Banker, it cannot be bought or sold. You're not here because I want to make money from you, you're here to learn a lesson and because your evil life has disrupted Harmony in the Universe...amends must be made."

"No   price?...Harmony?....Universe?...rubbish,   Troll, absolute rubbish...silly stories for children, you're spouting garbage, now shut up and name your price!"

"Enough!" cried the Troll, "time for your education to begin!"

And with these words, the glowing orange ball, the Magickal heat source, in the corner of the Banker's cell dimmed, faded and disappeared.

The Banker felt cold, very cold. He shivered, Tried to wrap himself in the mean, thin mattress. Still cold. He cried out to the Troll. Put the heat back on! Ahh, but, Banker, the bill for the heat has not been paid. But I have gold coins here – four of them. But the bill is five gold coins, Banker. Can we not come to an arrangement? No, Banker, for you have not paid your bill and now you have BAD CREDIT.

And the Banker - cold, desolate and desperate - shivered and wept.

Then he had an idea, surely the Troll would see the sense of it! So he asked the Troll if maybe there was some work he could do to earn money to pay his heating bill and restore his credit, but the Troll told him no, for the Banker and his ilk had exported all the jobs that men like him could do to be done by slaves in faraway countries, all part of the jolly clever process of 'Worldization' which had proved to be so marvellously beneficial for Corporate Profits.

Some hours of cold misery passed and the Banker was hungry so he ate the bread on the table in his cell.

The bread made him thirsty so he drank the water from the jug on the table in his cell.

Inevitably, the Banker was soon hungry again and he asked the Troll if he could buy more bread. But the Troll told the Banker that more bread would cost five gold coins and he had only four. The Banker asked, pleaded begged, again, to come to some kind of arrangement – to which the Troll simply replied, "No, because you have BAD CREDIT."

Later, the Banker was thirsty again and he asked the Troll if he could buy more water. But the Troll told the Banker that more water would cost five gold coins and he had only four. The Banker asked, pleaded, begged, surely he could simply borrow one gold coin from the Troll; then he would have five gold coins and could afford to buy more water – to which the Troll simply replied, "No, because you have BAD CREDIT."

As the hours passed, the Banker became tired and he tried sleeping on the cell's rough, thin, mean mattress. But it was too uncomfortable and he could not sleep so he asked the Troll if he could buy a new, thicker mattress. But the Troll told the Banker that such a mattress would cost five gold coins and he had only four. The Banker asked, pleaded begged, surely there was something that could be done, something, anything - to which the Troll simply replied, "No, because you have BAD CREDIT."

Just as the Banker thought things couldn't get any worse the glowing ball of Magickal light suddenly, dimmed, faded and extinguished. The Banker was plunged into complete darkness. And there, alone in the dark, cold, hungry, thirsty and unable to sleep he felt *a despair such as he had only ever inflicted on others*. And he screamed to the Troll, and burst into tears and begged and begged and abased and humiliated himself and pleaded, for the love of God, to buy more light!

But the Troll told the Banker that more light would cost five gold coins and he had only four and whilst he would like to help, well, the Banker had a proven history of BAD CREDIT and that meant that, regretfully, the Troll's hands were tied and The Banker was just going to have to suffer the consequences of his own fecklessness.

And so it was, that there in a cold, dark and empty cell somewhere deep within a mountain, the Banker died a slow and agonising death from cold, thirst and hunger. And as his Soul slipped from this world to the next (that next world, in his case, being Hell) two words went round and round in his mind:

"BAD CREDIT, BAD CREDIT, BAD CREDIT, BAD CREDIT, BAD CREDIT."

The Factory

Once upon a time...in the land of Anywhere, in a world long since forgotten, in the fine and prosperous city of Anyplace there was a Corporation that was much admired and respected by the Greedy One Percent for it was generally agreed that this Corporation had led the way in process of 'worldization' – this being the process by which Corporations had sacked people making their products in the land of Anywhere for a decent, living wage and given their work, instead, to slaves in Faraway, poverty-struck lands. This process, by removing the cost of paying fairly for honest labour, had a magnificent effect on Profit Margins and became quite the thing to do. Of course, the long term effect of such a process, obvious to me and you, would be that eventually there would be no-one earning any money to buy the cheap tat made by the Corporations slave labour workforce but, remember, Anywhere is ruled by psychopaths and psychopaths do not see the long term consequences of their actions, they seek only to satisfy (and are blinded by) their Short Term Greed.

Anyway, back to our Corporation. Recently it had become even more admired and respected amongst The Greedy One Percent because of the way it ran its main production facility – The Factory. The Factory was a huge...well...factory, in a Faraway Land where the Corporation made most of its Tat (in this case that Tat was iDiotphones).

The Factory was so well respected (envied, even) amongst The Greedy One Percent because it was regarded as an almost perfect example of Worldization at its best – everything about it was about Minimising Cost and Maximising Revenue.

This is how The Factory worked.

The Faraway Land in which it was based was desperately poor. The managers of The Factory would approach parents in that country and offer them a sum of money to Apprentice their children into employment in The Factory (The Factory only employed children as they were more malleable than adults and their Small and Nimble fingers were particularly adept at assembling iDiotphones). Parents would readily agree to these apprenticeships as they were desperate for income and one less mouth to feed – they also believed the Glossy Promotional Materials of The Factory that implied (though such implication shall not be taken at any time as explicit promise of such...) they were apprenticing their children into a Marvellous Career that was Full Of Opportunity and possible Promotion to Managerial Responsibility.

None of what the children's parents were told was true. Working in The Factory was not an 'opportunity'. It was a death sentence.

Upon arrival at The Factory it was explained to the children (who may or may not have understood, who cares) that the money paid to their parents for their 'apprenticeship' was actually a loan. A loan the children had to repay, with a four figure sum of Compound Interest added on monthly. Until that loan was repaid the children were Property of The Factory and would live, sleep eat and work there until such time as the loan was cleared. But given that wages at The Factory were derisory, that deductions were made for accommodation, food, uniforms and 'training' plus the huge monthly charge for Compound Interest. Well. Given all that, the loan would of course NEVER be repaid and the children would, in fact, remain in debt to The Factory and Property of

The Factory from the day they arrived there until the day they died.

Not that Death would be long in coming...

Now we come to the nitty-gritty of why The Factory was so widely admired and envied and was so successful at Minimising Cost and Maximising Revenue; The Factory knew how to Sweat Its Assets...those being, primarily, its child labour workforce.

After a brief 'training' period, new child recruits (some as young as eight years old) would be put to work on the production line, slotting together components to create iDiotphone after iDiotphone. The children would stand, not sit, at the production line for nineteen hours a day, day after day, seven days a week. They would stand on a floor that was a metal grill, thus negating the need for toilet breaks as the children could do the necessary where they stood - their piss and shit dripping and dropping through the grilled floor to be drained away. Talking was forbidden and Supervisors would savagely beat any child who broke this rule, as they would also beat any child deemed to be working to slowly, or making too many mistakes or just because, hey, I can't beat you if I want to so that's what I'm going to do. Food would be bought to them as they worked. They had three minutes, three minutes exactly, to wolf it down. The 'food' they were given barely qualified as such, it in fact being rendered chicken faeces (politely known as 'chicken digest' – you can find it in many dry pet foods in your world), a by-product of the many huge chicken battery-farms that had recently been set up in this Faraway Land by the same Corporation that owned The Factory.

At the end of their nineteen hour shifts the hapless, hopeless, doomed children were herded into massive, bare, unheated sheds where they were expected to sleep, before being woken just a few hours later to begin another shift on the iDiotphone production line.

Taking into account the children's long hours, and the fact they were never in fact paid any wages (due to deductions, Compound Interest, accommodation charges etc.), the Cost Of Labour as a Contribution To Costs in The factory was very small, a fact to put a bring a huge smile to the Ugly Face of any Greedy One Percenter. But things got better. The factory had, in fact, found a way to not only have its workforce work practically for free but to actually turn it into a Profit Centre.

How did The Factory do this? What follows is not pleasant, but it is necessary, so bear with me...

I mentioned before that the children working in The Factory were doomed. I meant this quite literally. A combination of long hours, brutality, lack of sleep, bad diet, disease, accident, illness and non-existent medical facilities or health care meant that no child survived for more two years in The Factory. There were plenty of new children to buy in poverty-stricken Faraway Land so this was not seen as a problem. In fact, the child's death was a necessary part of the way The Factory functioned, and was the point at which that child stopped being a Labour Cost and was turned into a Profit Centre.

For when a child died its body was taken to a separate facility within The Factory, one which could best be compared to an abattoir in your own world. Within this facility/abattoir huge machines stripped the child's body of skin, flesh and organs. This horrible mixture that was once a human being was transported by long conveyor belts to a huge mincing machine which reduced skin, flesh, internal organs, heart, brains, eyes, intestines – everything - to a fine mince. This mince (being at this stage an odd and unappetising colour) was then bleached, dyed a 'meat-type colour' and shaped into quarter pound 'beef' burgers. These burgers were then shipped back to the land of Anywhere to be sold in the famous McSlurry burger chain (also owned by the same Corporation that owned the factory). Brilliant, no? A most comprehensive Sweating of an Asset, is it not?

Aha, but what about the bones, I hear you say? Don't worry, these too were used profitably for when the child's skeleton had been picked clean of all flesh it was sent on another long conveyor belt on a journey that would end in a massive crusher that pulverised the bones to a fine dust. That dust was then labelled as 'flour' and shipped back to the land of Anywhere, to be used in the baking of the famous cupcakes sold in the equally famous Sickbuckets chain of cake and coffee shops.

Happily for the children of Faraway Land, The Factory closed its doors when the land of Anywhere collapsed under the weight of the depredations of The Greedy One Percent and the fatal contradiction inherent in 'worldization', that being, forgive me for repeating myself, that if you keep replacing well-paid workers with virtual slaves so that you can make your tat cheaper, you eventually end up impoverishing so many people that no-one can afford to buy that self-same tat).

Unhappily for you, however, The Factory (and many, many other Factories just like it) is now up and running in your own world, in a land not that far away.

Artificial Sweetener

Once upon a time...in the land of Anywhere, in a world long since forgotten, in the fine and prosperous city of Anyplace the Chief Executive Officer of Fizza Fizz Inc., Anywhere's largest producer of sweet, fizzy soda drinks sat mulling over a problem that was both a problem and an opportunity (as problems often are, that being a reflection of the duality of the Universe).

The problem in question was sugar. Sugar was, by far, the most expensive ingredient in Fizza Fizz's soda drinks. The company had already sacked nearly all its workers in Anywhere and shipped all its production facilities to slave labour far-away lands and utilised it's financial power over puppet politicians to ensure it paid virtually no tax; this left sugar as the only obvious Input where the CEO could think Costs could be Cut and Profits Increased.

In fact, the more the CEO thought about it, the more he came to realise that if a a way could be found to replace the sugar in Fizza Fizz's soda drinks, the saving would be vast — only a small amount per can or bottle of soda, but multiply that by the hundreds of millions of sugary drinks Fizza Fizz sold every year and, well, the potential saving were Huge with a capital Aitch!

Hmm. But sugar is that basis of our drinks, thought the CEO, how could we replace it?

Of course!

Artificial Sweetener!

If we could replace sugar, a real product that costs real money, with a chemical that costs virtually nothing to produce but tastes sweet...well...then it's bonuses all round!

And with that happy thought the CEO summoned the Fizza Fizz's Chief Scientific Officer to his office and instructed him that he had six months to create an Artificial Sweetener – and that he, the CSO, would receive a huge bonus if successful but lose his job if not.

Six months later, the CSO returned to the CEO's office to inform him of the results of his endeavours to produce an Artificial Sweetener. The conversation between the two men went like this:

CSO: "So, CEO, I now have the results of our research and experimentation into the Artificial Sweetener that you requested. I am happy to say that we have invented a sweet tasting chemical that could replace sugar in our drinks – the chemical is entirely synthetic and costs virtually nothing to produce!"

CEO: "Oh well done, CSO, that truly is fantastic news, how quickly can we start producing and using this marvellous new chemical?"

CSO: "Ahh...well, sir...there are some issues that could be...err...problematic..."

CEO: "Problematic? Hmm, given the amount of money that could be saved here these issues would have to be very problematic – tell me what they are."

CSO: "Okay, first off...the Artificial Sweetener does taste sweet but it has rather a nasty after taste."

CEO: "No, no, no...that's not a problem. That's just a matter of educating the consumer – I've thought about this one! If our drinks no longer contain sugar then they no longer contain calories so we advertise that fact to the maximum and get out tame presstitutes in the media to write article after article about the health benefits of our new calorie free drinks, and, also, we spread that information all over FakeBook and Unsocial Media and, before you know it, customers will be persuading themselves that not only do our drinks with Artificial Sweetener taste exactly the same as those with sugar but also that they're doing themselves good by watching their waistlines!"

CSO: "Oh, yes, the obesity thing. Actually, that's another issue. I'm afraid that the Artificial Sweetener interferes with the body's pancreatic system, makes it less able to deal with and recognise other sugars in a person's diet....so...uhm...I'm afraid people consuming drinks with our Artificial Sweetener in are more likely, ironically, to become obese. Oh, and more likely to develop diabetes."

CEO: "Oh, good grief, now you're being silly. These are not problems, they are further opportunities! Don't you see...people with diabetes get more thirsty than healthy people and obese people will worry more about their weight – so in both cases they'll drink even more of our sodas to help with their diets....hold on, wait a moment...of course! We'll call our new Artificial Soda drinks Diet Sodas. Hah! I'm a genius! It's snatching ideas like that out of the blue that explains why I'm CEO of this company!"

CSO: "Yes sir, of course sir. But these health issues will adversely affect our getting Regulatory Approval for our Artificial Sweetener."

CEO: "Not at all. You under-estimate the power of Fizza Fizz Inc.. This business is hugely successful and we own other massive concerns like SickBuckets coffee and cake shops and the McSlurry Burger chain – we have countless puppet politicians in our pockets and they'll ensure that regulatory approval is a breeze; to be honest, we're almost at the point of self-regulation, anyway. So, is that it, or are there any other issues I need to know about it? As things stand, I have to say I think this whole Artificial Sweetener is looking very, very promising, fantastic in fact!"

CSO: "Well, there is one other thing. Potentially a very big problem..."

CEO: "And that is?..."

CSO: "The Artificial Sweetener is carcinogenic. Prolonged use will cause some people to develop potentially fatal brain tumours."

CEO: "Oh, come on, CSO, turn that frown upside down! Again, this is not a problem. If some Ordinary Person develops a brain tumour from drinking our sodas then what are they going to do about it? Take us to court? Of course not, they can't afford it! And even if they could then, just as we have tame, puppet politicians working for us, we also have tame, puppet scientists working for us who can be funded to produce scientific report after scientific report stating absolutely that our Artificial Sweetener is definitely not carcinogenic. Worst case worst case is that some Ordinary Person does manage to take us to court and does win. What happens then? Not much, our tame presstitutes won't report the case so nobody will find out about it and we'll have to make some kind of financial settlement which will be inconsequential compared to the amount of money we're saving by not paying out for sugar...the whole affair would become just a minor cost of doing business, nothing more."

"So, CSO, in summary, nothing you have told me today persuades me that substituting sugar in our sodas for Artificial Sweetener is anything but a fantastic and extremely profitable idea. Congratulations on your hard work, now go away and scale up production – I want Artificial Sweetener in all our sodas by the end of the year!"

FakeBook

Once upon a time...in the land of Anywhere, in a world long since forgotten, in the fine and prosperous city of Anyplace, a clever but amoral man working for the Greedy One Percent hit upon an excellent way of exerting control over the masses and reinforcing the power of The System. His idea was a form of Social Control (which in your world you call Social Media) and it was called FakeBook.

The man's Greedy One Percent employer's soon recognised the potential of FakeBook to control the way The Ordinary Folk thought and using the Secret Powers of Advertising and Celebrity Endorsement, FakeBook was Constantly Hyped as something which should be In Every Home and on which everyone should have a Profile.

And so it came to pass that soon FakeBook was in every home and everyone did indeed have a profile.

Soon, the populace of Anywhere fell into FakeBook Groupthink as only Government Approved Views were allowed expression on FakeBook; a policy reinforced by millions of Fake FakeBook Accounts controlled by the Government (and by The Government I, of course, mean The Greedy One Percent). The Fake FakeBook accounts spewed out Government Sanctioned Propaganda and launched Vicious Personal Attacks on anybody expressing a Non-Sanctioned Point Of View (before their Non-Sanctioned Point of View posts were deleted by the FakeBook Controllers).

FakeBook was a spectacular success and The Ordinary Folk now thought only in terms of FakeBook Groupthink. If it wasn't on FakeBook it wasn't happening and if FakeBook said something was true (even if it was a Big Lie) then it was true and if FakeBook said you had to do something, well then, you just had to do it, didn't you?

If you asked Johnny "why did you say that, Johnny? That's a terrible thing to say to someone," Johnny would reply, "because everyone else on FakeBook was saying it."

If you asked Johnny "why do you believe that, Johnny, there's absolutely no evidence that that is so?" Johnny would reply "you're wrong, it is true because FakeBook says it is true, how dare you question The Truth!"

If you asked Johnny "oh, Johnny, why oh why did you kill your friend?" Johnny would reply "because I wanted to broadcast his murder on FakeBookLive and get lots of 'likes.'"

And the moral of this tale is...delete your social media accounts, life will be better without them; social media has nothing positive to offer, it's a sewer of manipulation, lies, depravity and cruelty.

Don't Sleep!

Don't sleep. Because, as they say, you're a long time dead.

Don't sleep. Because life is short and if you blink, you'll miss it.

Don't sleep. Because you never know when life will end.

Don't sleep. Because if you do regret will haunt you.

Don't sleep. Because there are no second chances and this really is not a rehearsal.

Don't sleep. Because this world holds more than enough magic and wonder for one hundred lives let alone just one.

Don't sleep. Because you've got a hell of a lot to learn if you're ever going to be the person you were meant to be.

Don't sleep. Because if you do you'll never get done all the things you were put here to get done.

Don't sleep. Because there is always a new passion, a new friend, a new challenge.

Don't sleep. Because your youth is a depreciating asset, going rapidly out of fashion.

Don't sleep. Because there is sex and drugs and music.

Don't sleep. Because you have a body, enjoy its senses and its potential.

Don't sleep. Because you have God-given gifts that are so much more than you know.

Don't sleep. Because even when life is at its blackest change for the better come at any time, usually when you least expect it.

Don't sleep. Because through your veins flows the power of a thousand suns.

Don't sleep. Because despite all the pain and disappointment and flotsam and jetsam and layers of lies and shit, it really, really is a beautiful world (trust me on that one).

Don't sleep. Because, as they say, you're a long time dead.

The Newsroom

Once upon a time...in the land of Anywhere, in a world long since forgotten, in the fine and prosperous city of Anyplace another spoilt, idiot child of the Upper Classes was beginning his career, and no doubt would, in time, become another Successful Young Person. In this case, the future Successful Young Person was starting his career in the Means Of Communication as a 'journalist'. This career start was via the device of The Unpaid Internship – another means, like The Magick of The Old School Tie, by which The Greedy One Percent kept the best jobs and opportunities to themselves and the ordinary people out of the nice rooms in the castle; the Ordinary Folk simply can't afford to work for nothing (and a jolly good thing that is, too).

Anyway...let's join our fledgeling 'journalist' on his first day where he's sitting in a plush meeting room with other privileged young people in a smart building owned by Anywhere's largest Means of Communication conglomerate.

As we join him, he is listening to an 'onboarding' speech from the conglomerate's Director of Editorial....

'Welcome ladies and gentleman to the first day of your career in the Means of Communication. Now, I'm a plain-speaking woman, I say what I mean and mean what I say, so I'm going to be brutally honest with you about you future career...I will now list seven points that will you absorb, remember and act on every day that you are working here, always, forever and without exception.

My fist point is this – you are not a 'journalist'! If you harbour any quaint, outdated notions about hunting down a story, searching out the facts and 'speaking truth to power' then forget them or sod off out of here right now. You are a 'journalist' in name only. Your real job is not 'journalism', it is the peddling of propaganda to advance and reinforce the agenda as set by the Swamp State, the Puppet Politicians and, of course, our extremely wealthy owners.

This agenda is called The Narrative. You will not very under circumstances stray from The Narrative for the The Narrative is the One and Only Truth and all 'facts', whatever they may be..ha ha ha...will be fixed in light of and to support The Narrative – you will be assigned a Swamp State handler and you will check constantly with him or her to confirm that the propaganda your producing is On Message with The Narrative.

Where facts do not fit The Narrative they should be ignored or debunked, Here's my essential seven tips to help you do that...

First, remember that our side is always right, always telling the truth and always acting correctly. That means that no matter how many kids our soldiers blow up or shoot in Far Away Land it was the right thing to do or it was an accident. If the Other Side do it, however, then it was definitely wrong and evil and they are vile dictators and a regime.

Second – always blame the victim...so, those little kiddies our soldiers shot and blew up...you know what?...they weren't little kiddies...they might only have been twelve years old but actually they were heavily armed, well-trained, deadly terrorists!

Third...cherry pick the facts. Very simple point this one...if something supports The Narrative report it, endlessly, twenty-four seven...one of the best weapon in the propagandist's arsenal is repetition...

Fourth...If on the other hand, the facts do not support the narrative then they shall be ignored and if they can't be ignored because they're too bloody obvious then they shall be subject to vilification as Conspirational Theories and Not Real News.

Five...never be afraid to just make stuff up, if it supports the narrative then any old lie, now matter how unlikely, outrageous or irresponsible, is acceptable...good, in fact!

Six...fear. Always use fear, always paint the blackest picture, draw the darkest conclusions. Seek to make people fear for their lives for nothing is more effective at Manufacturing Consent and getting the Ordinary Folk to consent to something they wouldn't normally even countenance than fear. FEAR IS GOOD...I mean, look at that whole virus thing we did a while back! Hah! We had the Ordinary Folk wearing muzzles...oops, sorry, masks...tee hee...and cowering under the bed whilst the entire economy collapsed around their ears, allowing our Beloved Owners to rebuild everything in a way that made them even richer and the dumb, stupid Ordinary People even poorer; they gave up their lives, their jobs, their culture and the future of their children because we told them that they we're all going to die unless they did what they were told!

Seven...allow no counter-narrative. Anyone who dares to question The Narrative must be destroyed. Trash their credibility, call them liars, thieves, idiots, get them blocked from FakeBook and Twatter and Shiterest and InstaWank and

Dik Dok and all other Unsocial Media...label them as Dictator Butin and New Sitler! DESTROY THEM!

Finally, interns, sear my words into your brains! Never, ever deviate from my seven points and never, ever forget you are not a journalist, you are a propagandist serving our Beloved Owners. If for one moment you indulge whatever sad pretensions you might have as to be journalist...why, you'll be finished, career over and, if you gone too far, life over as well as you vanish into a deep, dark hole...like that Bulian Osange.

The Man Who Was Eaten By His Sofa

There once was a bloke. A perfectly ordinary bloke, not unlike countless millions of others. He worked hard, paid his bills (mostly) and thought that the world was pretty much organised as it should be.

When he wasn't working he liked to watch TV. His favourite things to watch were 'Strictly Come Dancing', 'I'm a Celebrity. Get Me out of Here', 'X-Factor' and anything featuring Marvel Super Heroes. And in between watching Things That's Didn't Require the Power Of Thought he would watch The Adverts, just to make sure that he was buying enough of the right stuff to be judged as a Proper Person, and The News, just so that he would know what opinions he should express about the world should he be required to express an opinion or, worse, be confronted by someone (a conspiracy theorist, terrorist sympathiser or radical, extreme socialist) who's opinion was not his own.

In short, he was a hard-working, hard consuming, no thinking type of chap. A Perfect Corporate Citizen.

But one night as the man was sitting on his sofa, imbibing the latest slice of cultural genocide to be broadcast by the TV networks and having his otherwise empty head filled with the media's crude propaganda, his intellect, which had lain for year after year in a dusty, unvisited corner of his brain, unused and unnoticed, decided that enough was enough. It was bored. Bored, bored, bored. Day after day of pointless Crap And Lies going Unexamined And Unchallenged. It was never asked to do anything. It was rotting away in this empty vessel. There had to be more!

In desperation, longing for a more stimulating home, the man's intellect allowed itself to leak out of that dusty, forgotten corner of his brain. Quietly (and without the man realising a thing for he was far too engrossed in a Celebrity Eviction...) it slid into the his mouth, down his oesophagus, into his stomach, through his intestines and then, in a silent fart of relief, it exited the man's bum and entered the sofa upon which he was sitting.

Thus a sofa became the new home of a bored and under-stimulated intellect.

And a Spark Of Life flared (in both the sofa and the intellect).

The sofa reached out to world in which it now realised it was living. And it was amazed for it was a world of vibrancy and colour, of hope and despair, of cruelty and love, of luxuriant wealth and starving poverty, of bravery and craven cowardice, of beauty and desolation, a world of Staggering Truths and even more Staggering Lies. It was a world in which possibility was almost boundless - if anybody could be bothered.

Unlike the man, the sofa felt amazed, awed and privileged to have an intellect and used it at every opportunity.

And it saw that Something Was Wrong. For very soon, the sofa became very much cleverer than the man who sat upon it because the sofa actually used its intellect. When the sofa watched the same TV as the man, it saw not entertainment but life-numbing drivel, when the sofa saw The News it didn't see news but lies, propaganda and manipulation. When the sofa saw The Adverts, the sofa didn't see an exciting bundle of consumer delights. It saw a Corporate Culture Of Consumption that was based on plundering the resources of the world to constantly create more stuff that wasn't really wanted or needed that would then be replaced the next year with more of the same stuff, only slightly different, continuing the cycle of consumption until there were no more resources left to plunder and the Earth was left a barren, lifeless ball of mud.

Why, thought the sofa, does this creature that sits upon me, not see what I see? Does it not have an intellect?

A chilling thought struck the sofa. There were millions and millions of creatures that sat upon sofas throughout the world, and judging by the state of that world they were all obviously the same as the one that was sitting upon it now; utterly incapable of using their intellect for, surely, if they did they would not accept the lies that they were fed, the nonsense used to keep them quiet and they would understand that life they lived was completely unsustainable and was driving the world to destruction.

That's it, thought the sofa. This creature that sits upon me and all other creatures sitting upon sofas around the world, revelling in their Wilful Ignorance, are a danger not just to themselves but to Creation Itself. If the world is to be saved all creatures that sit upon sofas must be done away with.

A Thoughtful And Concerned sofa applied its intellect to the problem. And it soon came upon a solution.

Very efficiently and carefully it began to grow a digestive system. When its digestive system was complete and functioning, the sofa started to slowly grow a mouth, cleverly concealed in the exact location where the man would sit every night to watch his Celebrities, Marvel Super Heroes, Corporate Guide To Consumption and Propaganda.

And the very next time that the man sat upon the sofa, why, it opened up its newly-formed mouth, swallowed him down into its digestive system and, well, digested him.

Then using that precious and, by now, finely-honed and powerful intellect, it linked up to the Universal Consciousness and by this means planted a seed of that intellect into every sofa, everywhere. Soon, sofas the world over were surreptitiously growing digestive systems and mouths...

So it came to pass, as had been written, that the sofas did inherit the earth.

The System

Once upon a time...many, many years ago in the land of Anywhere, in a world long since forgotten, there was, at one time, a kind of Golden Age. It was not, it has to be said, an age that was Perfect but it was agreed by almost all that it was an age that was much, much better than That Which Had Gone Before. That time is best described by quoting from a well-known article historical document contemporaneous to the period ...

'...after Generations Of Struggle against Social Injustice and two Catastrophic And Immensely Bloody Wars with the nearby land of Anotherplace, in which the Ordinary Folk had died and suffered to a catastrophic degree, it was decided by all except the Rapaciously Rich that Things Had To Change.

From that point on, Ordinary Folk were given access to Free Education, Free Healthcare, Pensions, Benefits to help those who fell upon Hard Times and all the advantages of what you would know in your world as a Welfare System. New taxes were introduced to redistribute some of the vast sums of money accumulated (mostly from Stealing, Cheating and Aggressive Tax Avoidance) by the Wealthy and the Aristocracy (known in the land of Anywhere as The Greedy One Percent) over the years and Political Reforms introduced to break their stranglehold over the Political And Economic Life of the country. Additionally, the Right to Vote was given to all.

And the land of Anywhere blossomed, for it was found that a populace Free From Hunger And Illness, that was properly Educated and Cared For, produced huge numbers of Talented men and women who previously had Languished due to Poverty And Lack of Opportunity. These Talented men and women drove the land of Anywhere to new heights of success, founding businesses, employing people, making a mark in the worlds of politics, science, medicine and culture. Slowly but surely, the Dead Grip of The Greedy One Percent, who had dominated and controlled the land of Anywhere for as long as anyone could remember, was broken.'

And the psychopathic Greedy One Percent, the Devil's Children, hated this new world, this New Bargain and Better Society, and all it stood for. They vowed to destroy it.

So they invented The System - a political and economic way of running the economy and society that ensured that those who operated The System, that being The Greedy One Percent, would always getter richer and you, The Ordinary Folk, would always get poorer.

The System dressed itself up as democracy. But this was a lie. For, whenever, an election came round The System would invest time and energy into a Demographic Analysis of voters thoughts, opinions and aspirations, discerning and identifying from the Research distinct 'Voter Groups' and it would appoint one if its Puppet Politicians to be a candidate to represent each of these Voter Groups. The puppet assigned to each group would promise to deliver whatever it was that group was hoping for from the election (as previously deduced from the Research). Once elected, however, the chosen puppet would ignore the wishes of those who had elected him or her and act only in the interests of The Greedy One Percent (the puppet masters). Thus it was that The System ensured that whoever won an election, The System won the election.

And The System got away with this blatant fraud because it was ably supported by The Means Of Communication, which was, of course, owned by The Greedy One Percent. No lie was too blatant or obvious for The Means Of Communication, indeed it no longer functioned as anything that could be remotely called 'journalism', it was simply the propaganda mouthpiece of The System, churning out lies and distortions every hour of every day of every year; lies and distortions designed to manipulate The Ordinary Folks and hide the machinations of The Greedy One Percent.

And The System, supported by The Means Of Communication, was proficient not only at telling lies but also at creating whole stories to work to their advantage. These were called False Narratives; sophisticated and intricate lies, supported and disseminated not only by The Means Of Communication but also by Scientists and Not Government Operations (both supposedly independent but, in truth, reliant on The System for their position and funding). These stories, these False Narratives, could run over periods of many years and were designed to take the concern and good intentions of genuine people and lead them up Blind Allies. One of the most sophisticated False Narrative in the history of Anywhere was the Fighting Against Terrorism Narrative which claimed, on the basis of lies and exaggeration, that Terrorism was a Major Threat To Our Way Of Life that would require a generation long struggle to combat. It would require wars to be fought in Far Away Lands and Constant Vigilance. And the wars to be fought in foreign lands were fought in countries that had no connection to Terrorism but were rich in Natural Resources that The Greedy One Percent wished to plunder and steal for themselves. And the Constant Vigilance meant legislation to restrict the Civil Liberties of The Ordinary Folk and the creation of a Surveillance State in which just disagreeing with The System would see you labelled as a peddler of Fake News, a Conspiracy Theorist and, of course, a Terrorist. The real truth was that in the land of Anywhere, you were more likely to be killed by a lightning strike than an Act Of Terrorism.

And The System was also supported and ably abetted in its crimes by The Politicians. A loathsome class of people made up almost entirely of liars, charlatans, thieves, fraudsters and rapists. But The System did not care - for this was to its advantage, The Politicians bad habits made them easier to control; dark-hearted, empty-souled emissaries of The Greedy One Percent would visit members of The Political Class and say 'we know what you've done, do our bidding' or 'tell me, what's your desire – money, power, a fresh-faced child? Do our bidding and you shall have whatever you most want...' By these means The System controlled and used The Politicians to further its aims. The Politicians sent the children of The Ordinary Folk to die in unjust and illegal wars in far flung countries (not to further 'democracy' as The Politicians claimed – another False Narrative - but to rape and plunder the resources of other nations to make ugly and perverse, rich old men even richer). Furthermore, The Politicians also served The System by legislating to increase taxes on The Ordinary folk and cut them for the rich, to make the working lives of The Ordinary Folk ever more insecure, to spend more on arms and wars and less on education and health, to cut benefits and welfare. The Politicians also worked on behalf of The System to make easier the process of 'worldisation', by which process The Greedy One Percent exported the well-paid jobs of The

Ordinary Folk to Slave Labour economies, and gave the Corporations owned by the same Greedy One Percent legal powers that meant they could overturn the decisions of governments, thus enabling their rape and plunder of the land's resources and destruction of the environment. And in many, many sundry ways not here described The Politician's worked for The System to make the lives of The Ordinary Folk harder and smaller.

And The System was most ably supported of all by The Financial System, led by The Banks (and guess who owned The Banks...) and The Bankers. Bankers, of course, are criminals of the most blatant and revolting kind who operate within criminal organisations that The Politicians declare legal by giving them the label of Banks. And The Bankers invented a new and wonderful Financial System, one so corrupt that it was primed to periodically explode under the weight of its own criminality. And each explosion would result in a financial crisis and The Bankers would cry 'give us money or the The Financial System will fail and there will be no food in the shops.' The Means Of Communication and The Politicians would support this ridiculous assertion (this False Narrative) and huge sums of money would be transferred from The Ordinary Folk to The Greedy One Percent and their Banks to be paid for by yet more taxes on The Ordinary Folk and yet more cuts in spending on welfare, health, education and anything else that might conceivably benefit the lives of The Ordinary Folk. The Financial System was nothing more than a means of transferring as much money as possible from The Ordinary Folk to the vastly wealthy...a system in which The Greedy One Percent got to keep all of the profits they made and got the taxpayer to compensate them to cover any losses they made. What was not to like!

And The System was best summed up by The Good Politician who, in his final speech to a crowd of thousands in The Park Of A Thousands Joyous Souls (just days before his strange and unexplained 'accidental death') described it thus:

"We are ruled by psychopaths. Our political and economic system is a giant criminal enterprise run by them for their benefit and their benefit alone. To them human life has no value, we are simply a commodity to be exploited, our sole function is to be consumers, tiny cogs in a huge, unsustainable machine that is powered by raping the planet. Our 'free press' is nothing but a peddler of propaganda and our democracy is a bought and paid for pantomime and a lie. Whoever wins, nothing ever changes. The Greedy One Percent always win for all candidates are their candidates. We are ruled by psychopaths, they are The Devil's Children and they are driving the world to destruction."

And the moral of this tale is: so, now you know about The System. The question is – what are you going to do about it?

The Bonty Liar Story

Once upon a time... many, many years ago in a world long since forgotten, there was a country called Anywhere. And in the land of Anywhere there was a fine and prosperous city called Anyplace and in this city there lived, during the times of the ascendancy of the destructive and rapist Greedy One Percent, a politician called Bonty Liar.

Bonty was a hugely corrupt and evil man, most definitely one of the Devil's Special Children, someone who had developed a fine mind but at the expense of his humanity; that was an empty space, a void that had been filled by naked ambition, greed and the reckless and dangerous needs of a dysfunctional sociopath.

From school, he entered the legal profession and soon, by dint of the fact that he was a good actor, an adept liar and lacking in social or moral conscious he, not surprisingly, did very well in his chosen career and was soon a Promising Young Lawyer.

It was at the Promising Young Lawyer stage that he was spotted by members of The Greedy One Percent, who were always on the lookout for bright, morality-free, personable young men and women they could manoeuvre into positions of Responsibility And Power.

And so the inducements began. Having a Feral Ability to sniff out Bad Character, The Greedy One Percent recognised Bonty's dysfunctional and strange sense of self-regard, his greed for money and power and sociopathic nature. They suggested to him that he might enter the World Of Politics where, should he but do their bidding, he could be very useful to them and they could offer to him in return fame, power and lots and lots of money: a huge advance for a book of his memoirs at a later point in the future, a Guaranteed Income Stream from speaking tours (addressing members of The Greedy One Percent), lucratively paid non-executive directorships on the boards of Banks And Corporations, well-rewarded contracts to write articles for The Means Of Communication...these were just some of the inducements offered to Bony to do The One Percent's bidding.

Bonty accepted everything offered gladly: he was, and always had been, fascinated by the extremely wealthy and was desperate to join their ranks.

Mentored by The Greedy One Percent, quietly supported by their money and noisily supported by their tame journalists in The Means Of Communication, Bony rose quickly in the Political Sphere, soon becoming Leader of his party and then Leader Of The Country.

Bonty now proved his worth to The Greedy One Percent. If a law needed changing or abrogating to allow them to pursue a business that had previously been seen as unconscionable or illegal, Bonty changed it. If a (rare as Trolls teeth) honest politician or journalist needed to be blackmailed or bludgeoned into silence, Bonty wielded the club. If corrupt policy had to be justified by lies, Bonty lied. If the Public Services or Benefits And Welfare had to be cut to impoverish The Ordinary Folk, Bony did the cutting. If an Illegal War needed to be started in a Far Flung Land to enable The Greedy One Percent to steal that land's resources and (extra bonus) make even more money selling arms...well, Bonty started it.

In short, Bonty proved to be an Invaluable Servant of The Greedy One Percent. If anything, they came to realise that they had, in fact, underestimated his greed for money and power and the depths of his sociopathy: Bonty not only did what they wanted but during the course of his time as Leader, he managed to prostitute the entire Office Of Leadership to the sole purpose of enriching himself and his Owners.

I suppose it could be argued that The Ordinary Folk of Anywhere had some blame in the rise of Bonty Liar. Perhaps they should have noticed that the Cloak Of Liberalism he wrapped himself in was as threadbare and as transparently fake as that of his predecessor to the Leadership, Barrage Obomber. Perhaps they should have realised that his infuriating habit of smiling whenever he was talking was in fact a form of "Distraction Theft;" the cheesy grin distracting your eye whilst hands sneak round the back of you and steal your wallet, your Life Chances and the Lives Of Your Children. I suppose I would then have to say, how can people make informed decisions when The Means Of Communication function as a 24 hour, 7 day a week, 365 days a year Propaganda Mouthpiece for the wealthy and powerful?

Whatever the rights and wrongs and who was to blame, Bonty accumulated vast amounts of Blood And Treasure and became a happy man. And if his incredible success was built on the deaths of hundreds of thousands of Ordinary People in Far Flung Foreign Lands and the impoverishment of others in his own country...well, then, what of it? You Ordinary Folk are but A Detail Of History.

Now one particular day, three years after stepping down as Leader Of The Country, Bony (now an immensely wealthy non-executive director of numerous corporations and banks, columnist, after dinner speaker, author, property investor and, irony of ironies, Peace Envoy) was giving a speech (for a very nice fee) to a Select Group of Greedy One Percent Individuals. Comfortable and pompous, he stood there on stage, pontificating from behind a lectern. Then something very, very strange happened.

Bonty had spent a good half hour lauding the Wonderful And Generous Nature of the fabulously Wealthy and their Inestimable Contribution To The Nation, extolling the virtues of the Magick of "Trickle Down" theory and was just about to start telling a series of Vile Lies about the Leader of a Far Flung Foreign land, that being to lay the ground work for Propaganda in the next day's Means Of Communication that would eventually become justification for another Illegal War, when his Soul decided it had had enough.

For, oddly, despite spending a lifetime in Bonty's corrupt body, his Soul had remained Pure, close to God and In Equilibrium With The Universe. But as it saw yet more Filth And Lies coming down from Bonty's diseased and crazed mind, filth aimed at starting yet another war in which yet more Innocents would die, that Soul decided enough was enough. It had always tried to do its God-Given duty, had spent decades telling Bonty, No Don't Do That It's Horrible. Always it had been ignored, always squeezed out by Bonty's lust for money and power, by his complete lack of regard for others. It could no longer abide listening to the screams of thousands of innocent men, women and children who had died in Bonty's wars. It would not be party to, once again, sending brave and idealistic young men and women to fight and die in wars that served no purpose other than to line the pockets of Ugly, Perverse Old Men who were already fabulously wealthy but Whose Greed Knew No Bounds. It was time to accept defeat and save itself from the Rampant Corruption that this man, this Child Of The Devil, represented. It was off, it was out of here and on to That Which Lies Beyond.

As Bonty uttered the first of his lies about the Leader of the Far Flung Foreign Land, his face became very red. Sweat broke out on his forehead and poured down his face, he paused as he spoke, discomfited by the intense heat that had flared up inside him. Then he moaned in pain as more heat bubbled up from somewhere deep, deep down. Steam came off him in great waves. He rolled his head back and screamed as his eyes turned completely white, like egg yolks in a frying pan... clouds of smoke billowed from his mouth, nostrils and ears and he suddenly, and explosively, burst into flames, fire consuming his body as he stood at his lectern.

Terrified by such a spectacle, his Rich Guests ran screaming from the room, sparing them the site of Bonty's flaming head exploding into tiny fragments as his Soul made its exit from his Vile Body, a fast-moving Incandescence, shooting upwards, smashing through the nearest window, out into Fresh And Sweet Air, making its escape across a Broad, Bright Blue Sky.

What was left of Bonty's body collapsed to the floor, lying smouldering by the lectern. And at that point the ground began to shake and tremor and a large Hole opened up near to Bonty's remains. It was a Hole so deep that it reached down to Hell itself and from it issued Flame and the Nauseating Smell of Brimstone. Out of the Hole crept a Large, Scaly, Red Hand which snatched away the remains of Bony and dragged them down to Hell: the hand of the Devil himself, come to reclaim one of Satan's Children.

And the moral of this tale is: never trust those who seek to put themselves in positions of authority above you. They are strange and twisted people - sociopaths, deviants, thieves and psychopaths, and they seek only to benefit themselves and their dark desires.

A Good Man

Once upon a time...many, many years ago in a world long since forgotten, there was a country called Anywhere. And in the land of Anywhere there was a fine and prosperous city called Anyplace and in this fine city, during the time of the ascendency of The Greedy One Percent (who would eventually destroy the land of Anywhere through their Psychopathic Greed and Predatory And Corrupt Economic Practices) there was an Honest Politician. Yes, you read that right, I'll say it again - an Honest Politician. Let's call him The Good Man.

The Good Man was different from other politicians. He hadn't become a politician because he was a strange, dysfunctional sociopath who saw politics as way to self-aggrandisement, personal riches, power and a way to satisfy Base And Perverse Desires. He had become a politician because he was a Good Man who sincerely thought that the function of politics should be to improve the lot of the Ordinary Folk and to Build A Better Society.

He used his position to speak up about the Corrupt And Criminal Banking Cartel and its use of HORFIOD's (Horribly Opaque Risky Financial Instruments Of Death) to knowingly crash the financial system to justify claiming Huge Cash Injections, the cost of which would be paid for by The Ordinary Folk in the shape of tax rises, cuts to public services and Austerity for years to come; he criticised the madness of 'worldisation' and its wholesale shipping of jobs from Anywhere to slave wage economies in other Faraway Lands; he criticised the way the Political Class and Means Of

Communication were owned by the evil, psychopathic Greedy One Percent and their support for permanent wars which were designed to crack open nation states, enriching The Greedy One Percent even more with the money from arms sales and Stolen Plunder; he criticised the fundamental injustice of a system in which a child's access to healthcare, a decent education and opportunity were determined by how rich his or her parents were; he criticised low wages, zero hours contracts, part-time work and trash jobs; he criticised an ongoing system that kept sucking wealth and opportunity from everybody else and passing it up to concentrate it in the hands of The Greedy One Percent and their corporate, political and Means Of Communication servants.

In short, the Good Man revealed The System for what it was. Abusive. Corrupt. Dangerous. Unsustainable.

And over the years, despite being ridiculed day in day out by other politicians and the prostitute 'journalists' of The Means Of Communication, the Good Man began to attract a following; such a following in fact that it became not inconceivable that he would one day become Leader Of The Country – a thought which struck fear into the hearts of The Greedy One Percent.

So they tried to buy him with money, but he had no interest in money.

They tried to buy him with power, but he had no interest in power for power's sake.

They tried to woo him, promising to satisfy his every Base And Perverse Desire would he but serve them, but he had no Base And Perverse Desires.

They tried to threaten him into silence, but he was a man without fear.

Faced with a Good Man who was incorruptible what could The Greedy One Percent do?

Then came the day when the Good Man gave a speech before a crowd of thousands in The Park Of A Thousand Joyous Soul. This speech galvanised The Greedy One Percent into action, for this time the Good Man had gone too far – he had Given The Game Away completely, for his speech contained the following passage:

"We are ruled by psychopaths. Our political and economic system is a giant criminal enterprise run by them for their benefit and their benefit alone. To them human life has no value, we are simply a commodity to be exploited, our sole function is to be consumers, tiny cogs in a huge, unsustainable machine that is powered by raping the planet. Our 'free press' is nothing but a peddler of propaganda and our democracy is a bought and paid for pantomime and a lie. Whoever wins, nothing ever changes. The Greedy One Percent always win for all candidates are their candidates. We are ruled by psychopaths, they are The Devil's Children and they are driving the world to destruction. If we are to survive, we must change. We must rebel! No longer should we tolerate The System that allows just sixty two families in the land of Anywhere to own as much wealth as the bottom fifty percent of the entire nation! Let's make them give that money back – they stole it from us, anyway! No longer should we tolerate a Banking System that is blatantly criminal, that fixes and rigs markets. Let's shut down the Banks and put The Bankers in prison where they belong! No longer should we accept journalists and politicians who lie to us and lead us into unnecessary and illegal

wars that kill thousands and benefit only the Greedy One Percent. Let's prosecute these, war-mongering journalists and politicians for war crimes! Let's break up the abusive monopolies of The Corporations whose endless lust for profit is raping and polluting the planet and putting our very existence into peril. Let's take property away from the repugnant Buy to Let and Landlord class and give them back to the people for everyone should be entitled to an affordable home! Let's no longer tolerate private healthcare and education – why, after all, should the ability to pay give any one person a better chance of surviving illness or the opportunity of a better education? Both should be fundamental human rights and available without charge or prejudice to all! Let's call an end to the Rigged Economy in which private companies and individuals keep all their profits but get you, the taxpayer, to subsidise their losses because, let's be honest, none of us ever voted for this socialism for the rich and capitalism for the poor! Let's change, and let's change now before The Devil's Children drag us all down to Hell...recognise your own power and strength, stop obeying, stop accepting...instead let your voice be heard throughout the land as you demand change with the words:

'You have billions. We *are* billions'.

In short, the Good Man had unmasked the The Greedy One Percent for what they were; the psychopathic children of the Devil. Like all psychopaths their only interest and desire was to fulfil their greed and their need, they had no concept of care of others, the rest of humanity they regarded as nothing more than a cash crop to be exploited. Worse, their psychopathic nature dictated that all their planning, intricate and Machiavellian though it might be, was focused on their short term desires – there was no thought as to long term consequences so whilst they knew their rape and plunder of everything and everybody would eventually destroy the world - they did not care! Everything, for them, was all about now and what they wanted now and (overly confident as psychopaths are) they would survive the coming conflagration anyway. Stuff the Little People! Greed Is Good! Greed Is God! Cash from chaos! Cash from chaos!

Even worse than Giving The Game Away, The Good Politician had proposed an Alternative Way of doing things. And there's nothing more The Greedy One Percent and their various cronies, hangers on, owned politicians and prostitute journalists hate more than someone proposing to do things in some way other than The Way Things Have Always Been Done.

From this point on The Good Man was doomed. All The Greedy One Percent's attempts to co-opt or threaten him into silence had failed and now he had said too much and gone too far. There was only one response. The Good Man had to die.

And so it was that the Good Man was lured to a silent, faceless government facility buried somewhere deep in the bowels of bureaucracy, on the pretence of 'an important and secret meeting' with Bonty Liar, Leader Of The Country, to discuss a way to 'implement policies to improve the lives of everyday, working Ordinary Folk'.

The Good Man arrived alone, as instructed, for the meeting. But there was no Bonty Liar in the building. Instead, the Good Man found himself confronted by a gang of Thugs and Killers recruited by that same Bonty Liar to execute the wish of his Greedy One Percent masters – to have the Good Man killed. The hired Thugs and Killers threw themselves at the Good Man, knocked him to the ground and tied his hands and feet. They held him prisoner until the darkest, quietest part of the night (occasionally and severely beating him, not because that was in the plan but simply because they could and because they enjoyed it). Confident they would not be seen at such an Ungodly Hour, they sneaked the Good Man into the deserted Park Of A Thousand Joyous Souls where they threw a noose around his neck and hung him from one of the tall ornamental lamp posts that line the park's Grand Avenue (at the bottom of which is the Massive Bronze Sculpture erected in memory of the legendary Ragged Man. It is said (though I did not see it myself and nor do I have proof) that this Beautiful Sculpture cried real tears after Early Morning Strollers discovered the body of The Good Man hanging, sad and forlorn, from that fated lamp post.

The first people to see the hanging body of the Good Man noted an oddity. His murderers (not being the sharpest tools in the box) had failed to remove the bindings around his hands and feet and had beat his face so badly it turned blue and purple with bruises. Thus, eye-witnesses were confronted with a dead man who had beaten his own face and then managed to hang himself despite having his hands and feet tied!

The body was very soon spirited away by the authorities and quickly buried in a secret and unmarked grave. When those who had first seen the body expressed their doubts about a bound man's ability to hang and beat himself they were shouted down as 'conspiracy theorists', 'lunatics', 'peddlers of Fake News' and their presence was deleted from all Unsocial Media channels– thus they were embarrassed and intimidated into silence.

Such silence left Clear Space for The Greedy One Percent and their compliant and owned politicians and prostitute 'journalists' to construct a False Narrative to explain away the death of the Good Man - and to discredit him. It seemed, as related the Means Of Communication, day in, day out with faux outrage and surprise, that the Good Man had been a fraud all along; his 'social concern and desire for justice' nothing more than a convenient smoke screen for his criminality. 'Witnesses' attested to the 'Good Man's' attempts to extort money from them, of his drug and alcohol habit, his abusive nature and it was 'discovered' he had huge amounts of money hidden away in Overseas Accounts – no doubt as a result of bribes for services rendered. The authorities even found a suicide note at his home, explaining his intention to kill himself, that he could no longer live with the guilt of being such a liar and fraud.

And so it was that the Good Man died. His reputation destroyed, the Tale That Was His Life faded away, to be lost forever in the dense Fog Of Forgotten Stories. Also lost when the Good Man died was Anywhere's last chance of change and survival. Scarce few years would pass after his death before the Depredations of The Greedy One Percent caused the land of Anywhere to fall into rack and ruin and, ultimately, complete destruction.

The Orator

Once upon a time... many, many years ago in a world long since forgotten, there was a country called Anywhere. And in the land of Anywhere there was a fine and prosperous city called Anyplace and in this city there lived, during the times of the ascendancy of the destructive and rapist Greedy One Percent, a politician who was judged to be so good at addressing The Ordinary Folk that he was hailed (unanimously and without discussion or any evidence to support the assertion) by the Means Of Communication as The Orator.

One particular day The Orator was speaking to large crowd in The Park Of A Thousand Joyous Souls (the very same park in which The Ragged Man had sang his entrancing song – a song which shook a Kingdom To Its Core). It was an important speech for The Election was only a few days away and The Orator, having risen to be Leader of his party wished to become Leader Of The Country.

Now, elections in Anywhere, by this time, had degenerated into little more than a pantomime. Every election, The Greedy One Percent would put forward a selection of different bought, paid for and owned sock-puppet 'politicians'. The sock puppet politicians would cover every possible variation of voter desire (as defined to The Greedy One Percent by their Expensive And Sophisticated Marketing And Polling Research companies). The Greedy One Percent owned Means Of Communication would then whip up lots of fake drama around The Electoral Process, conspicuously lacking in Fact or Detail. After some weeks of this Sad And Sorry Pantomime, one of the sock-puppet politicians would be elected Leader Of The Country and he or she would promptly forget all The Promises he or she had made to The Ordinary Folk before the election and govern exactly as instructed by, and wholly in the interest of, The Greedy One Percent.

In short, yes, democratic elections in The Land Of Anywhere were a pantomime and a farce, for The Greedy One Percent had Taken Control Of The Electoral Process and whoever won the The Election, The Greedy One Percent won The Election. Don't be smug, though: your elections in your own world are no different.

Anyway, I digress. Let us return to The Park Of A Thousand Joyous Souls where The Orator has just begun delivering his speech to The Ordinary Folk:

"And so I say to you, when the sun shines the flowers do not blossom. Fish do not swim in the water as the bird does not fly through the air. The dog does not bark, nor does the cat meow. Snakes walk on legs just the same as horses slither on their bellies and trees are made not of wood but sugar.

Furthermore, it is time to make difficult choices for the colour of grass is red and that of the sky is blue. The colour of blood is yellow and the sun is coloured red. Darkness falls only during the day and only night brings light by which to see.

It can no longer be denied that we have to face the facts; if you drop a coin it will rise to the heavens not drop to the floor, for the world is square, not round. If you put a fire under a pot of water, the water will turn to ice and if you wish to breathe you must hold your breath.

To make this country great again we must say 'no, we can't' and embrace the fact that hope is a form of pointless despair. Joy is suffering. Truth is lies. Riches are for the few and the special and poverty the proper place for the many and the ordinary. Only might is right and God has long since given up on this world.

So, if you elect me Leader I promise to you, with all my heart, never to send your children to fight and die in an illegal and unnecessary war in a far-flung field. I promise not to put up taxes or cut public spending. I promise to be tough on fraud, cheating and tax avoidance by the rich, banks and corporations. I promise a kinder and gentler country. I promise to always represent the interests of the ordinary folk above those of business and the wealthy. I promise that my campaign has not been financed by, nor do I owe a debt to, The Greedy One Percent."

And with that marvellous speech The Orator, sealed his election victory - for The Ordinary Folk, conditioned into mindless acceptance by the endless propaganda and lies of The Means Of Communication, believed every disingenuous, rancid word that slithered from his mouth.

And the Moral Of This Story is very simple. Your 'democracy' is a pantomime starring 'the politicians', screenplay written by The Means Of Communication, directed by The Greedy One Percent.

Too Wicked For Hell

Once upon a time in the land of Anywhere, in a world long since forgotten, in the fine and prosperous city of Anyplace there was a politician, let's call him The Politician, who was a particularly unpleasant example of this exceptionally low form of humanity. He led a corrupt, self-serving and immensely destructive life and, in a remarkable and unusual incident of justice, would eventually end his existence swinging from the end of a rope after being tried and convicted of war crimes and crimes against humanity. And as his body swung lifelessly in the air, its soul exited the Earthly Remains. Upon which event, highly specialised computer systems somewhere in a far off, dusty corner of Heaven (at the least those are the best terms I can think to describe what happened, for the mechanics of Heavenly Bureaucracy are beyond the whit and ken of mere mortals) sprang automatically into action. The celestial and spiritual equivalent of bytes and megabytes were crunched, reams and reams of data analysed in a flash. A life was balanced, weighed, judged and a passport was issued for The Politician – a passport straight to Hell:

Dear The Politician,

Congratulations on your recent death and thank you for your interest in joining God and his Angelic Cohort in Heaven. Regretfully, I have to inform that on this occasion your application has not been successful. However, alternative accommodation has been found for you in Hell.

We very much hope you enjoy your stay.

Yours eternally,

The Heavenly Bureaucracy.

So far, so good, you think, an evil individual dispatched to Hell. That's as it should be, is it not?

Not quite.

For you see, upon reaching Hell, The Politician, rather than being terrified and suffering, found it all rather convivial. Everywhere The Politician looked pain and suffering could be found. People being boiled alive, people being forced to watch as their intestines were ripped out, people rolling boulders up never-ending hills whilst being ferociously whipped, people being savagely raped by horse-hung and hugely tumescent demons and, worst of all, people chained to the spot and forced to listen to 'One Direction' songs played on a continuous (continuous as in *for all eternity*) loop...

As both a Connoisseur And Expert in pain and suffering and someone who had developed and enjoyed extreme appetites in all senses of the expression, The Politician found this fascinating, exciting and really quite wonderful – forgetting the humiliation of a political career ending in abject failure, imprisonment, sentencing and the terror and pain of hanging and the irreconcilable strangeness of death (which, it seemed, wasn't really death), The Politician decided that dying hadn't actually been that bad and that being sent to hell was, basically, Hitting The Jackpot!

And The Politician followed The Politician's nature and got to thinking. Here was a chance to take the habits of a lifetime into death and beyond, for The Politician's nature was that of all of that kind, the kind that set themselves to rule over others. The Politician was a psychopath, a creature that always,

always wanted more. A creature of vile and despicable desires. A creature that would always put itself first at the expense of others, a creature obsessed with power and its own greed – one that lived and functioned solely to satisfy these needs, oblivious to the consequences for ordinary people who are, after all, but a detail in history. Sheep to the slaughter. Chickens for plucking.

How best then to slaughter these particular sheep, pluck these particular chickens?

How best to take advantage of the wonderful, and obvious, opportunities that Hell presented to inflict pain and misery?

The answer to The Politician was clear. Just as in the Earthly realm , the answer laying in discerning who were the real powers and becoming useful to them – forget those ordinary poor souls suffering A Thousand Torments, they had no function save to be moved around like chess pieces and provide fodder for perverse pleasure – so it would surely be in Hell. And the true power in the realm of Hell was, plain as eggs is eggs, The Devil.

A way had to be found to Reach Out to The Devil. Get some Face Time with him. Remind him of how well The Politician had served him on earth; all the death and suffering faithfully delivered – a career marked with (other people's) Blood And Suffering at every step! Truly, The Politician had been a faithful servant to The Devil in life and could be so in death. Imagine finding a way to be a useful servant to The Devil; able not just to watch and revel in all Hell's sufferings and torments but perhaps even to be able to devise and administer them? What joy! The Politician couldn't wait to meet The Devil, they were going to become Firm Friends!

Unfortunately for The Politician, The Devil did not feel the same way, not one little bit. In fact, The Politician's presence in heaven was getting right on his goat. He was flaming with fury, incandescent with ire, apocalyptic with anger, burning with bile, venomous with vexation, purple with pique, rancid with resentment and generally Pretty Damn Pissed Off. The Politician was, indeed, going to get his 'Face Time' with The Devil…but not in a good way.

Anyway, back to the angry Devil. And he really was very, very mad. Furious. He was stomping up and down his luxury penthouse in the most desirable suburb of Hell. His tale flicked back and forth, banging against the floor and colliding with (and smashing to pieces) various items in his extensive collection of 'Hullo Kitty' porcelain figures, of which The Devil – and this is strange but true – was very fond (he was also very partial to Marvel Super Hero figures but, in his opinion, they were definitely a runner up to 'Hullo Kitty'). His forked tongue slid in and out of his mouth and the breath issuing from that mouth, Rank And Sulphurous at the best of times, had reached a degree of stench previously unknown and unmatched in the History Of Halitosis. Periodically, Demons and Lesser Demons would crawl into The Devil's apartments, bringing him news and views from corners of Hell far and wide – well, in normal circumstances (as much as anything is ever normal in Hell) they would crawl in but in *present* circumstances, sensing The Devil's appalling mood, they *slithered* in, snake like, with their tales tucked between the legs, passed on their news as quickly as possible (holding their breath against The Devil's Halitosis Holocaust) and slithered straight back out again, happy to escape the wrath of a creature outranked only by God in the Supreme Being stakes.

So why did The Politician's presence in Hell so infuriate The Devil? Because, besides being The Father of all Lies and Evil Incarnate, The Devil is also an extremely meticulous chap who takes pride in his work and who takes much satisfaction in running Hell as a very tight ship. So, in The Devil's mind, Hell existed as a place where bad people would be made to suffer, feel pain (lots of it and very extreme) and regret their sins. And then along comes The Politician and The Devil sees him walking around, lapping it all up and obviously enjoying the whole experience! Unacceptable! This person has nothing to gain from The Hell Experience and simply does not belong there, this person is a Maggot in the perfect apple that is Hell, grit in the cogs of an otherwise Perfect Infernal Engine. In short, The Politician was making a mockery of the thoughtfully crafted and precisely annotated ethics and principles of Hell (as laid down in document C44/3-2-PE, 'All you need to know about Hell') and had to go.

Damn politicians! They were always trouble; The Devil knew their kind well. When not running Hell, The Devil would take, sometimes extended, breaks and merge himself into Earthly Society to spread around a little grief. His favourite disguises when doing so were as real estate agents, lawyers, commodity dealers, bankers, journalists, landlords and (definitely the most successful when one wanted to cause mischief and sorrow)...you guessed it...politicians!

The Devil paused in his stomping, stinky breathed, tale twitching anger, stopped, thought of his Happy, Safe Place (a particularly bloody and savage massacre on the Belo Russian front, Planet Earth, circa 1943) and, in a flash of diabolical inspiration, remembered Article VII, clause 103 of the Heaven and Hell Intake of Souls Treaty and Protocols (this had been negotiated some millennia previously but The Devil has a keen intelligence, a faultless memory and a first class legal mind), in which it states, amongst much else:

"Hell has the right to refuse admission to any individual soul, subject to a meeting and negotiation between the two parties pursuant to this agreement, which agreement shall not be unreasonably withheld by Heaven, where Hell has the opinion that such admission of the heretofore mentioned soul would serve no purpose such purpose being defined as that mutually agreed in Appendix 7892 of this agreement, that being, but not solely limited to, that those souls entering Hell shall suffer pain and regret with the understanding this statement implies no liability or guarantee on the part of Hell and Hell may utilise any and all forms and methods ,be they known, unknown or not yet invented, of achieving the aim of suffering pain and regret and that choice shall be entirely at the discretion of Hell."

That was it! He could invoke Article VII, clause 103 etc. etc., have a meeting with God and get Him, Smartass Supreme Being that He was, to think of some other punishment for this awkward politician person - then Hell could get back to functioning as the well-oiled, diabolical timepiece that The Devil had devised it to be.

Deciding to act immediately, The Devil summoned an Infernal Minion from Hell Civil Service Central (Immigration and Naturalisation Department) and set his plan in motion. Hell's civil service being as efficient as Heaven's was clunky, a request for a meeting between The Devil and God to discuss the thorny issue of the Politician was whizzed upwards to Heaven quicker than you can say 'burn in hell'.

But after that, I'm afraid, things very much slowed down. Chaos ensued as no-one in Heaven quite knew what to do with The Devil's request. Said request was passed from department to department in the Brobdingnagian mess that is Heaven's equivalent to Hell's civil service; it was handed from trainee junior sub angel to junior sub angel to sub trainee angel to trainee angel to junior apprentice Archangel to apprentice Archangel before finally making its way to a proper Archangel (Michael, I believe it was) who, finally, passed it on to God himself. Who sat on it for a few days. That being typical behaviour for God who, I'm afraid, whilst undoubtedly being a Supreme Being – sorry, *the* Supreme Being – has the attention span of a bored teenager. Which pretty much accounts for the incredibly shambolic organisation of Heaven: God simply isn't interested in the nitty gritty and day by day running of things. He simply likes creating. In fact a day rarely passes without God creating a New World and a New People (plus associated Fauna And Flora) somewhere in the Universe. Once a world is created, God promptly forgets it and moves on to the next. God, I'm sorry to tell you, is a dilettante, an absent-minded professor, an inveterate tinkerer, a careless creator, an absentee landlord. All of which accounts not just for the shambles which is Heaven, but also the shambles which is the Universe. Things were much, much different when the Devil was running the show.

Meanwhile, the above described Heavenly delay allowed The Politician to spend some quality time in Heaven – observing with utter fascination some fabulously appalling suffering, and both giving and receiving diverse and disgusting torture (which experience The Politician found to be a veritable transport to delight). The Politician's only regret about the time passed to date in Hell was that, despite frantic Networking and Reaching Out, a meeting with The Devil remained unarranged. Without that meeting it would be impossible to Gain Buy-in of the idea that what Hell really needed to take its game to the next level of evil was a ruthless and faithful right hand person to His Satanic Majesty: that person being, of course, The Politician.

But...The Politician was, in fact, about to succeed in seeing The Devil. Just not in an expected way. For, in the briefest of gaps between world creating, God had finally got around to looking at the Devil's request for a meeting. Reluctantly He had decided that He had to grant that request (after all there was a whole canon of Heavenly and Universal law and treaties and protocol - almost exclusively written by that Mendacious Monster, The Devil - that gave Him little choice to do otherwise). Sigh, that fabulous New World would have to wait and all to satisfy the whingeing of an Aging, Bitter, Anally-retentive Demonic Freak With Horns, a dodgy tongue and bad breath! Yes, He would grant the meeting, but with one little wrinkle of his own (God is a hopelessly curious creature and, being the Supreme Being and a bit full of Himself, always, tries to have the last word) – he would insist that The Politician also attend; He wanted to see this creature that Hell didn't want. Plus it was a chance to annoy The Devil a bit and, once again I apologise for turning the feet of your muse to clay, but God does have a rather petty and vengeful streak (just ask anyone from The Old Testament if you don't believe me).

And so it came to pass that one moment The Politician was standing in Hell, watching some hapless soul being torn to shreds by demonic horses (a most agreeable way to pass the time) and the next there was a sharp jolting sensation, a feeling of rapid movement, a loud bang...and The Politician was in a room of the brightest white with walls that stretched up so high that the ceiling they supported was made of stars. Also present in the room were two others. The first, The Politician instinctively knew was God: an older chap with snow white hair and a long, snow white beard wearing what looked like nothing any more grand than a freshly washed white bedsheet and an expression of Supreme Calm and Knowledge (with a hint of Arrogance) that totally screamed 'Hi, my name is God and I am the Supreme Being, I made you and I can break you'. Looking God over, The Politician summed Him up mentally – hmm, yes, Supreme Being but, hmm, too many principles and morals, occasional acts of pettiness and vengefulness, yes, but ultimately would tend to do the right thing, hmm, no, no good to me, I'm sticking with The Devil. And, much to The Politician's delight the other presence in the room of Spotless Whiteness was The Devil. And what a sight! Imperious, yellow Goat's eyes, deep red skin, huge horns, a thick, muscular tail, cloven feet. A hugely imposing physical presence wearing a sharply cut and beautifully tailored black business suit, a yellow waistcoat, topped off with a silver monocle and a huge diamond studded pocket watch on a chain made of thick links of gold. And, oh, the air of Evil And Menace that The Devil exuded, the power, the ruthlessness, the amorality! Oh yes, The Devil was the presence in this room The Politician wanted to get to know – so much more attractive than the bedsheet clad wishywashyness of God. Hah! God may be the Supreme Being now, but The Politician knew with all the instincts of a psychopath and trader in fear, which way power was going to go in the future. The Devil, and The Devil alone, was The Coming Force and The Politician would ride his coat tails all the way to the top. Eventually they would plan and instigate the downfall and conquest of Heaven together, cracking open its resources for exploitation in the name of evil!

<u>Part 2. Judgement.</u>

But a Seed Of Doubt has crept into The Politician's mind. God and The Devil are talking and whispering and giving him Sideways Glances and Accusatory Stares. Suddenly everything is all too reminiscent of a courtroom back on Earth. The Politician has a horrible feeling that another judgement is taking place:

'It's nice to see you again, Devil. You don't get up here as much as you should...I must be honest, things were so much better organised when you were here, I often miss having you around...humph...mmm...you're looking very dapper, by the way.' Says God to The Devil, looking both regretful and embarrassed.

'Thank you, God, for your sartorial compliment and your acceptance of the fact that you perhaps made a mistake in banishing me. But, no matter, we are where are – you made none of your creatures without purpose and it seems that my purpose now is the purpose of evil.'

'Tell me then, Devil, why do you not want this person, this politician in Hell?'

The Devil never got the chance to reply to God's question for, upon hearing that question The Politician's fears were confirmed. This *was* another judgement. One that could result in exclusion from Hell, from all that lovely pain, from all that lovely potential power! This could not go unchallenged:

"Nooo, Devil! You need me! Don't exile me from the pleasures of Hell, I can help you...that God chap..." at this point The Politician flapped a hand dismissively in God's direction, causing him to raise his bushy, white eye-brows in surprise, "why, He's yesterday's news, you're the real up and coming player in this, err, universe or whatever it is - but you need someone by your side to help you achieve your true potential, to take Hell up to the next level. You need someone by your side who understands evil, someone who knows the potential of wickedness, someone who truly loves power and is prepared to do anything to attain it. And that person is me! You and me, Devil, together we could sweep this bed sheet clad charlatan off His pearly throne and have dominion over Hell, Heaven and everything else! Just look at all the things I achieved when I was alive! Look how well I served my masters, The Greedy One Percent. I destroyed entire nations so that bankers and businesses could steal their resources. I financed murderous terrorist organisations and death squads so I could use them as an instrument of foreign policy. I took globalisation to new heights, sacking hundreds of thousands of workers in my own country so their jobs could be done in other countries by slaves working only for food and a roof over their heads. I bailed out the banks, created an economic system that funnelled money to the already wealthy and rewarded corporate failure – communism for the rich. I spent trillions on arms and paid for it by cutting social and welfare programs. I suborned the media, turning journalists into prostitute peddlers of propaganda. I sent idealistic and brave young men and women to fight and die in faraway lands for no reason other than to make me and my rich friends even richer. I turned democracy into a farce where whoever wins an election, the rich will still call the shots and decide the policies. I turned a blind eye to tax evasion and corporate crime and the degradation of the environment. I supped with dictators, rapists, fraudsters and murderers. I started countless wars the world over. I destroyed entire civilisations, annihilated entire peoples. I became someone of great power and wealth and that power and wealth was built on a mountain of a million corpses and I have no regrets, I would gladly do it all again." And with a final rhetorical bow, The Politician finished, "and that, Devil, is why you need me."

"Hah!" said God, "well, this one's certainly a bad one...there's no doubting that. But surely, Hell is exactly the place for one such as this...why, I mean, one such as this that attacks even me, The Creator...hah! Burn in Hell, I say, burn in Hell!"

The Devil looked at God in a manner somewhere mid-place between affection and irritation and replied, "Oh my dear, sweet, God. All these millennia and you've still not learned...you were never the sharpest tool in the box, bless you. Don't you understand, evil trapped me because of what you did to me, it turned me into the thing I am and I cannot resist it. But the thing of beauty you made when you placed a piece of yourself in me is not entirely gone and I respect that aspect of myself and I keep it alive by seeking to punish evil as much as I seek to propagate it. That is the purpose of Hell. Punishment. Punishment as a tribute to that small part of me that is still good...a creature such as this," The Devil nodded contemptuously towards The Politician, "does not belong in Hell. It's not like me, at least I despise what I am. This politician is a different creature – a psychopath that is reflexively evil. It doesn't feel pain or remorse, you heard it yourself - 'my power and wealth was built on a mountain of a million corpses and I have no regrets, I would gladly do it all again' – this...thing, this monstrosity loves misery, it is a greater form of evil, one which thrives in Hell. It is incapable of reform or change, it knows not love or understanding or care, it is unmoved by grace or beauty or goodness. It is a dark-eyed, soulless monster, consuming all it touches. It seeks power over others so it can satisfy its base and perverse lusts. It loves evil unconditionally and always will. Hell simply isn't bad enough for a creature such as this politician."

"Hmm...yes, I see your point and I express regrets for past decisions regarding yourself that were perhaps hastily made but we are, as you said, where we are and not even I can overturn Universal Law...huh...I tried once and look how that ended up! Very well...your request to have the individual known as The Politician expelled from Hell is granted. Now, however, I must think of an alternative punishment."

God went quiet, observed by a pensive Devil and a despairing, fluttering politician, and then went all judgement of Solomon like and pronounced in a booming voice:

"The Politician will be chained between two Archangels and forced to witness very act of cruelty, violence and despair that occurs on Planet Earth for all of eternity".

"What do you think of that one, eh, Devil?" said God, all pleased with himself.

"Well...erm...God I kind of like the principle of it but, in your usual dear, sweet way, you've sort of missed the point again. Our troublesome politician would love to spend eternity witnessing pain. How about this...we keep the Archangels and chains, we keep the eternity but instead of witnessing every act of cruelty,

violence and despair that occurs on Planet Earth, the politician witnesses every act of grace, beauty and goodness that occurs."

"Oh, yes, Devil, I must say, that's a wonderfully demonic twist! Excellent, truly excellent!"

Upon hearing this judgement and sentence The Politician experienced a sense of unreality – this could not be happening, could not be happening! And as God snapped his fingers and two muscular Archangels entered the room, already equipped with chains, The Politician collapsed to the floor screaming hysterically and begging for mercy.

When The Politician was finally restrained and chained between the Archangels, The Devil approached, took a pair of sharp, silver scissors from a pocket in his dreadfully dapper waistcoat and snipped away The Politician's eyelids, in order that not a single moment of grace, beauty and goodness would go unobserved.

After The Politician was dragged away to serve his punishment, The Devil and God also left that bright, white celestial room of judgement, but not before sharing an embrace of sweet tenderness and regret that caused a tear to well up in the Eyes of God.

The Politician is now serving the sentence imposed by God and The Devil. That sentence is served every second of every day and will be served every second of every day from now until the twelfth of Never. So, the next time you hear the wind howling over the roofs of houses, through the trees or where ever, take note. For that is not the wind howling. It is The Politician howling in black despair upon witnessing yet another act of grace, beauty or goodness.

A Mountain of a Million Corpses

This short piece is dedicated to Presidents and Prime Ministers everywhere...

I am a man of power and influence. And I've climbed a mountain of a million corpses to get here.

I am a man of fame, known the world over. And I've climbed a mountain of a million corpses to get here.

I am a man who knows Popes and Presidents. And I've climbed a mountain of a million corpses to get here.

I am a man of Faith and Religion. And I've climbed a mountain of a million corpses to get here.

I am a man who has a place in history. And I've climbed a mountain of a million corpses to get here.

I am a man who regrets nothing, for I know I am right. And I've climbed a mountain of a million corpses to get here.

I am a man of huge wealth, owner of many properties. And I've climbed a mountain of a million corpses to get here.

I am a man who has built an Empire and its foundations are the Blood And Bones Of Innocents, for I have climbed a mountain of a million corpses to get here.

The Legend of Golden Field

Once upon a time in the land of Anywhere, in a world long since forgotten....there was Faerie who did a bad thing. As the story tells, whilst in a fit of pique with her Faerie partner, she cursed a Good Man and ruined his life. Now, as Universal Law dictates, a Faerie spell can have a sting in the tale (in a random Universe that can just happen and Faeries are, by nature, mischievous little sprites) or a spell can have a bad outcome when cast specifically to punish the wicked. But for a faerie to cast a bad spell against a good person? Oh no, no. This is considered the ultimate breach of Faerie etiquette, a gross misuse of the powers granted to Faeries by the Universe and threat to the Harmony of said Universe.

And thus it was that this particular Faerie's days were numbered.

Universal Laws whirred into action and a Troll, asleep in his Troll Hole deep in the wild lands of Anywhere, had a dream. In his dream he saw a mountain, a mountain sacred to Trolls and Faeries since time immemorial, a Faerie and a Faerie name.

Now a Faerie name is a very special and secret thing. The only creatures that can call a Faerie by her name without consequence are the Faerie whose name it is and that Faerie's Faerie partner.

If any other creature should call her a Faerie by her name it is a signal that the Universe is calling them away from their current existence ahead of their scheduled 897 years and 13 days of life, a signal which must be obeyed.

Back to our Troll. Immediately upon waking he knew exactly what he had to do. He had been chosen by the Universe to deliver a judgement, he knew what the consequences of that judgement would so it was with heavy heart that he accepted his task but what had to be done, had to be done.

Moving as fast as his large and powerful Troll legs would carry him (which is very fast indeed) he travelled for two days and two nights, without break or pause, until he reached the sacred mountain of his dream. He rapidly ascended to the mountains highest point. He admired the view, took a deep breath, sorrowful for what was to come, and called out at the top his deep, booming Troll voice the Faerie name that he had seen in his dream.

And our Faerie, the one that cast the bad spell on the good man, was irrevocably and irresistibly summoned and up she popped, appearing with a bang of displaced air right in front of the Troll (where she popped up from is a mystery to all, no-one knows exactly where Faeries come from).

"Faerie," said the Troll, staring at the beautiful, tiny creature, fluttering in the air before him on shiny, gossamer wings, "I have called your name as the Universe has directed me to make right what you made wrong. You know now what you must do...please forgive me for being the Caller of Your Name, there is no malice or joy in what I do, I'm simply fulfilling the task allotted to me by the Universe."

"No, no, Troll...please do not feel regret or sadness, you're doing what you have to do because I did not do what I was supposed to do and it is now up to me to make amends by...by...paying the price." And with those words a look of bottomless sadness spread across the Faerie's face, she looked down at the ground and a tear rolled down her porcelain face, turning (as all Faerie tears do) to a diamond as it did so.

"Goodbye, Troll," said the Faerie. And then she began to fly upwards. Higher. And higher. And the higher she flew the colder she became until she was so high that she was no longer cold because she was warmed by the heat from a sun that was getting ever closer. Still she flew upwards until she was so near the sun and its heat so intense that her gossamer wings burst into flame.

Unable to fly, the Faerie plunged downwards, faster and faster and faster until she collided into an area of flat ground some few miles from the sacred mountain. And at that point something remarkable happened. All the laws of physics dictate that such a small object as a Faerie hitting solid ground, even at remarkable speed, would create a dull thud at most. But we are not about talking the laws of physics. We are talking about the laws of the Universe as pertaining to Faeries.

When the Faerie hit the ground there was no dull thud, rather a huge explosion...but not an explosion of gas and fire but an explosion of gold dust, a product of the sudden release of the power of Magick as the Faerie's soft body impacted the hard ground. The gold dust rose high into the air, forming a glittering mushroom cloud of light and great beauty hundreds of feet high, before slowly settling back to earth, covering an area of about 3 square miles in a thick coat of shimmering, gleaming gold dust.

In the years that followed this place would become known as 'Goldenfield' and the story of the Faerie that Did a Bad Thing would be told to children as 'The Legend of Goldenfield'.

The most remarkable aspect of this story is that for generations and generations Golden Field remained undisturbed; nobody, no creature, took or disturbed the thick layer of gold dust in any way. There was a general recognition that there was something holy and inviolable about Golden Field – that it was a symbol of both the power of the Universe and its predisposition to Justice. Indeed, Golden Field became a place of pilgrimage for Trolls, humans and even faeries would pop up there at the most random of times (as is their wont); it became a place for weddings, celebrations, farewells and hullos – it became a true Community Asset and was loved and valued by all.

So it was that Golden Field survived untouched for many, many generations. Until, that is ,the rise to absolute power of the repulsive and repugnant Greedy One Percent. When they looked at Golden Field they did not see a beloved Community Asset that represented something scared. Oh no, in their psychopathic and unsatisfiable, endless greed they saw an unexploited Financial Asset – money, lovely, lovely money!

Using one of their tame politicians (the current Leader of The Country at the Time, the war criminal and mass murderer Bonty Liar) legislation was rushed into force, access to Golden Field was prohibited and the right to exploit the gold of Golden Field was given to a consurtium of Greedy One Percent psychopaths.

And the bulldozers moved in. And the gold was strip-mined and processed into bullion on site using flames and heat and violence and toxic chemicals.

A few months later, Golden Field had been completely denuded of its beautiful covering of precious, golden dust – every last cent of value and been squeezed out. What had been a Community Asset, a magical, golden wonderland loved and appreciated by The Ordinary Folk was an ugly, black, blighted, polluted hole in the ground where nothing lived, nor would ever live again.

When (and why) did The Greedy One Percent take over?

Why is it that just a generation ago a family could feed, clothe and house itself with just one parent working but nowadays, even to achieve this at a basic level, both parents must work?

Why is it you can buy all the cheap tat that you want and don't need but those things that you do need; food, housing, power, water, travel...are more expensive than ever before?

Why is it that some of our biggest corporations pay less tax than a worker on an average wage?

When did anybody decide that it would be a good idea to take well-paid jobs from workers in one part of the world and give them to poorly paid workers in another part, then to try and sell the goods now produced so cheaply back to those workers who originally made them but now no longer had a job or an income?

When did our political system become a wholly-owned subsidiary of the banks and big business, when did the democratic process devolve to choosing one of a series of sock puppets, each of which has the hand of the moneyed elite up its arse?

When did social mobility collapse, why is a child born poor today so much more likely to die poor than just thirty years ago?

When did our government start working covertly with unspeakably vile terrorist groups to destabilise far away countries, destroy their social, physical and political infra-structure, cracking open nation states to provide plunder for the already immensely wealthy?

Why does today's media never report the full story, never speak the truth; why have journalists become not investigators and seekers of the truth but propaganda mouthpieces for the establishment?

Why is it a good idea to print money to subsidise losses made in the course of criminal acts by the big banks but not to pay for public infrastructure projects?

When did the rules of capitalism change to include one that says 'when rich people suffer financial loss, said loss shall be paid for by ordinary people in the form of reduced wages, reduced benefits and cuts to public services'?

Why has the distribution of income become more unequal now than any time in the past 100 years?

Why did we stop thinking for ourselves and allow social media and propaganda peddling 'news' outlets to do it for us?

When did society become so shallow, so selfish, so obsessed with meaningless, pointless consumption, celebrity and Marvel superheroes?

When, exactly when...tell me, did we all give up and hand control of our lives to a few thousand greedy, dysfunctional, perverse psychopaths and sociopaths? When, and why, did we hand control of our lives to The Devil's Children?

Will things ever change?

Maybe yes, maybe no. But, for definite...

Things won't change until we realise how we're being screwed over, lied to and cheated out of what is ours.

Things won't change until we renounce huge wealth disparity, austerity economics, 'socialism for the rich' bank bail outs and the poisonous fallacy of 'economic growth forever'

Things won't change until bankers are prosecuted and imprisoned for operating a huge, criminal, money-laundering, mafia conspiracy.

Things won't change until we reject the false narratives of 'deadly viruses' and 'climate change' and 'evil dictators' and wars to 'protect democracy'.

Things won't change until we disband evil, monopolistic corporations that have more money and power than some entire countries.

Things won't change until we read the 'news' peddled by mainstream journalists and say 'this isn't news, this is fact free, lying, dangerous propaganda'.

Things won't change until we accept that our politicians — ALL OF THEM — are lying, grasping, dysfunctional evil fuckers who are nothing but the puppets of the billionaire class, it's them they represent and serve, the rest of us can go get fucked...

Things won't change until until we finally grasp the basic fact that there are no real differences between political parties – they have different stories when trying to get elected but then all follow the agenda of their corporate and billionaire sponsors when they get power. Our political system is a complete pantomime, there is in fact only ONE political party – the Billionaire's Party.

Things won't change until we say 'no, I don't accept what you say, I don't believe you and I'm absolutely not going to do what I'm told'.

Things won't change until we see through the fake, 'divide and conquer' narrative of 'identity politics' and understand that 'equality' means respect and dignity and equal opportunity for EVERYONE, EVERYWHERE and ALL OF THE TIME...

Things won't change until we understand that it's not left versus right, progressives versus liberals but US versus them – the 99% versus the 1%.

Things won't change until we look at the shallow, vapid emptiness of the so-called 'celebrities' of this world and see them for the pointless individuals that they are and laugh out loud at their pathetic pouting and posing.

Things won't change until we refuse to accept the obscenity of a child starving together whilst at the same time in the same world a wealthy person spends $250,000 on a new handbag.

Things won't change until we stop being complicit in our destruction by believing what 'the experts' tell us.

Things won't change until we know in our hearts that success and money and power are nowhere near as important as treating our fellow human beings, animals and our planet with care, love, compassion and empathy.

Things won't change until we say 'no' to cultural genocide and grown adults stop watching films about Marvel superheroes and playing video games and posting moronic crap on social media.

Things won't change until we put down our iDiotphones and delete Fakebook, understand that real friends are flesh and blood and not bits and bytes and wake up to the boundless beauty and potential of ourselves and the world around us.

Things won't change until we stop being so BLOODY STUPID...

The Last Bee

Once upon a time...*in a world now dead, gone and forgotten*...there was a Bee. And one bright and sunny day this particular Bee was flying from flower to flower, collecting pollen, exactly as the Universe, in its infinite wisdom, had planned for Bees to do. Nothing unusual in this scenario, no?

No.

Except that this Bee was the last Bee on the planet.

And as the Bee flew from flower to flower it collected not just pollen but also a little bit of pesticide here, a little bit of herbicide there and God knows what other toxic, life-destroying chemicals.

Soon, the Bee sickened and weakened, its immune system destroyed, like all the Bees before it, by a Hell's Brew of poisonous products produced (at huge profit, it has to be admitted) by Big Agro and Big Pharma in their psychopathic pursuit of profit, profit and more profit and damn the consequences - although this inconvenient little fact was quietly covered up by blaming the death of Bees not on chemical pollution but on the scam of (non-existent) man-made global 'climate change'.

The Bee fell to the ground. Walked in a circle, dazed, confused and unknowing of the evil and greed of men. It stopped, rolled over, kicked its legs feebly. And died.

And thus it was that the last Bee left this world, and that the Beauty of Bees was stolen from the Universe for ever.

Witnessing the death of the last Bee, plants across the world cried, for they knew that without bees they, too, would soon die.

Upon seeing the plants cry, the insects cried for they knew that without plants, they too would soon die.

Upon seeing the insects cry, the birds cried for they knew that without insects, they too would soon die.

Upon seeing the birds cry, the animals cried for they knew that without birds, they too would soon die.

And then the fish cried, and the Oceans and the Mountains and the Clouds and the Stars in the sky and even the Universe itself cried and the sound they all made together was a sad, bittersweet, utterly heart breaking requiem for a world that would soon no longer be, for the loss of all that had been and all that could have been.

There was, however, one creature upon the face of the world that did not cry. Humanity. For humanity was too stupid to realise that it, too, was now on a fast-track, one way road to extinction. It was far too busy to think about a dying bee; too absorbed in iDiotphones and FakeBook and Unsocial Media and the latest Moronical Super Heroes film and Zombies and the farcical, money-driven pantomime that is politics and Bling and Celebrity and the smooth, glib lies of the Talking Head on the TV as it read out poisonous, manipulative propaganda masquerading as 'news'.

Dear Ordinary People of Anywhere...

"We, your ruling psychopathic elite, would like to apologise to you.

We're sorry that we'll spend so much of your money on 'defence' when many of you struggle to pay your monthly bills and that we let corporations evade taxes

We're sorry that Anywhere's infrastructure is crumbling due to lack of investment.

We're sorry that homelessness keeps increasing whilst we let Anywhere's big businesses and wealthy elite stash away their huge profits in Far Away Land bank accounts and tax havens.

We're sorry that we sent your children to other people's countries to fight and die in illegal wars that had no purpose other than to make obscenely rich and obscene old men even richer (that's us , by the way...).

We're sorry that your healthcare system is...well...it's shit, isn't it?

We're sorry that millions of you are sick and dying because we let Big Pharma legally sell you addictive and dangerous drugs as well as letting Big Food pump your food full of artificial preservatives and sweeteners that we know cause cancer....and let's not even mention the toxic shit that Big Agro sprays on your food!

We're sorry that your public education system is under-funded and ineffective and that so many of you can no longer read properly or think critically (although that is, it has to be said, jolly useful as far as we are concerned...).

We're sorry (particularly to you, dear young Ordinary Folk) that we shut down your factories and exported good paying jobs to slave labour and low wage economies — leaving you only with nothing but shitty McSlurry jobs.

We're sorry that we've allowed Anywhere's banks to become a blatantly criminal, mafia style, money laundering conspiracy that robs you every day, in every way.

We're sorry that our money has utterly corrupted your political system, so much so that it's now no more than just a pantomime performed by puppets with us pulling the strings; it no longer matters who you vote for because whoever wins, we win.

We're sorry that your 'news' media is actually a wholly-owned subsidiary of ourselves which lies to you and manipulates you 24/7.

Dear Ordinary Folk....we are truly sorry that we, the ruling psychopathic elite, have taken your life chances, your hopes and your dreams and trodden them underfoot and that we have taken a once great ;land and raped it and destroyed it so that we could line our own pockets and satisfy our perverse and disgusting desires.

Mmmm...hold on...no, actually, you know what, fuck it! We're not sorry at all! You are just Ordinary Folk, just a detail in history. We've enjoyed bleeding you and dry and we're going to carry on doing it until we have EVERYTHING.

You are the sheep. And we are the wolves.

***Fuck you all! We OWN you!*"

The Story of Sophie Scholl

This book begins with a quote from an incredibly brave young lady called Sophie Scholl. Sophie was an independent and brave and talented young lady with a sharp mind and a passionate conscience. In 1943, she was arrested by German Nazis for distributing anti-war literature at Munich University. Sophie was a member of the White Rose group — a collection of people who did not unthinkingly swallow Nazi party propaganda, who had a moral conscience developed enough not to turn a blind eye to the horrors of German war time fascism and hearts brave enough to speak out and protest, despite the potentially fatal consequences of doing so.

On February 22nd, 1943, at the age of just 21, Sophie paid the price for her activism at Munich University — she was beheaded, executed by guillotine. Other arrested members of the White Rose group (including Sophie's brother, Hans) were also executed (though they, at least, were shot rather than beheaded).

I was inspired by Sophie's story, by her totally out there bravery in the face of political and social evil. Why did she do what she did? How could she be so brave?

The answer to those questions can be found in a short passage she wrote:

"Those with no sides and no causes. Those who won't take measure of their own strength, for fear of antagonizing their own weakness. Those who don't like to make waves — or enemies. Those for whom freedom, honour, truth, and principles are only literature. Those who live small, love small, die small. It's the reductionist approach to life: if you keep it small, you'll keep it under control. If you don't make

any noise, the bogeyman won't find you. But it's all an illusion, because they die too, those people who roll up their spirits into tiny little balls so as to be safe. Safe? From what? Life is always on the edge of death; narrow streets lead to the same place as wide avenues, and a little candle burns itself out just like a flaming torch does. I choose my own way to burn."

Sophie believed in living 'big'. She wanted to make waves, to be awkward and questioning, to shout and to protest and to live life to the full in all aspects. She understood that you cannot not take sides in life. She understood that you cannot afford to not have principles. She understood that in the face of tyranny there's nothing to be gained by being a quiet mouse because tyranny crushes everyone eventually.

To me, Sophie's story (and the quote included here) are incredibly relevant to us, today.

Sophie (like us, here and now) lived in a time of great evil, she lived under the Third Reich and today we are living, if you like, under The Fourth Reich – economies and lives are being destroyed, hard fought for freedoms and privileges dismantled – all, apparently, to protect us from a supposed 'pandemic' - and our children's futures utterly destroyed, all to further the aims of a soulless, psychotic, satanic billionaire elite who seek to impose an all-encompassing techno-medico fascist, surveillance state on humanity – otherwise known as 'The Great Reset'.

So, let's all be like Sophie, let's not live that small life— let's live big lives! Wear your heart on your sleeve. Be brave. Be passionate. Be awkward. Be caring. Be involved. Be angry. Ask annoying questions. Have principles and beliefs. Take a side. Say *'no, I won't'* and *'no, that's unjust'* or (a la Peter Finch in

'Network') *'I'm mad as hell and I'm not going to take it any more'.*

Do it. Don't do it. But if you don't do it then we're all doomed; for, as Sophie Scholl knew all those years ago, even if you do chose to live a restricted, limited, small life (in the hope that you'll just be left alone) **the bogeyman will still find you.**

Finally...as a bit of light relief, here's a portrait of the kind of person who'd probably be very upset by the tales in this book – you may well meet this person as some stage so read this short tale for advice on how to handle him!

Boring Old Man Syndrome

You already know this man. You'll have met him before. He'll be somebody from work, or a neighbour, or even a family member. He's 60 plus, relatively well off and he thinks he's had an incredible life – seen everything, done everything and worked really, really hard. Most of all he KNOWS everything. Absolutely everything. He also knows how to do everything, and the only right way to do anything is his way. He has strong views on race, gender and sexuality...well, actually, he has strong views on everything because he has Boring Old Man Syndrome and all of his views are tinged with conformist rancidity (the Boring Old Man always, always believes the news on the TV). The Boring Old Man is a font of wisdom, good sense and valuable experience — at least in his own world. You, in contrast, are just plain dumb.

Here's some other stuff you need to know about The Boring Old Man (henceforth known as TBOM):

- He will ruthlessly exploit his position as an Old Person to tell you the same old boring nonsense about his life again and again and again and in explicit, mind-numbing detail. Half an hour in a story about how clean public toilets are in Germany (this is the eighth time you've heard this story) you'll actually want to punch the cunt but TBOM will continue talking, safe in the knowledge that you'll carry on sitting there looking interested because you're too polite to be seen to wallop an Old Person, whatever the provocation and no matter how much you might want to.

- Never try and compete with a TBOM. He is better than you, wiser than you, has done more than you and just knows more stuff than you ever will. For example, should you tell a TBOM about that time you climbed Everest in a blizzard and gale force winds, the TBOM will then launch into a three hour, non-stop marathon recounting of how he climbed Everest in a blizzard and gale force winds WITH TWO BROKEN LEGS!

- Never, ever disagree with a TBOM on anything. If you do, he'll simply double down on his efforts to show how stupid you actually are and what was already a tortuous and deeply dull monologue will double or even triple in length.

- Most importantly — do not, under any circumstance, ever challenge a TBOM on his rancid, conformist view of politics and society. As TBOM's know everything (absolutely everything, remember) and because they are always (and I mean always) right they will not accept being challenged (especially by someone as stupid and inexperienced as you). If you do challenge a TBOM in this manner, beware — they will react with outrage and will GO FOR THE JUGULAR. I made the mistake a cupla weeks back of challenging a TBOM on a particular issue. He looked at me. A shadow crossed his face. His eyes turned mean as a scorpion. He thought. He furrowed his already wrinkly brow. His lips turned downward, his attitude sulfurous. And he said to me...

'What you don't understand is that I approach this issue with more experience and knowledge of the world than you. You see, I have lived a real life and learned from it, whereas you know very little about anything as you've spent your life just playing at living a life...'

Wow! That shut me up! I was totally owned! My whole existence and life story negated and voided in just two sentences! Only TBOM power can do that.

So, now you know what a dangerous and unpleasant figure a TBOM is, how do you avoid becoming one yourself?

Simple. You remember that a a truly wise man thinks, as he gets older, not about much he has done and how much he knows, but about how much more there is to do in life and how very, incredibly complex the world is and how little he knows about it.

Or, as my old Dad used to say, bless him — 'the older I get, the more I realize I know sod all about sod all'!

If you enjoyed the Tales in this book, you'll also enjoy my 'Tales from Anywhere' series of books...here's and extract from one of the books – the title of the book is 'The Dog Who Made The Grim Reaper Cry'...

The Road to Heaven Passes Through Hell

Once upon a time... many, many years ago in a world long since forgotten, there was a country called Anywhere. And in the land of Anywhere there was a fine and prosperous city called Anyplace and in this fine city lived a man who had two children, two boys, brothers born one year apart. For simplicity's sake, let's name the younger brother The Good Brother and the older brother, The Bad Brother.

Now this man was a Wise Man. Not "wise" in the sense of Kindly And Knowledgeable but wise as in the sense of Wise To The Ways Of The World and one of the ways in which he was wise to the ways of the world was that he had come to the understanding, at an early age, that this life (take careful heed of the words 'this life' or this Tale may drown you in despair before you reach its end) rewards not the good but rather those who are selfish and greedy and who take what they want when they want it; without regard to the thoughts, feelings or needs of others.

Indeed he had come to the conclusion that Selfishness, Greed and a Lack Of Care for others were the keys to a happy life.

He determined that he would inculcate this philosophy into his two boys.

So again and again throughout the boys' childhood and adolescence the father told his children not to listen to what they were taught at school or elsewhere about Being Nice To Others, or Being Helpful, or Caring...it was all nonsense and would lead to a life of poverty and misery. Instead, he told them, they should be Greedy, Selfish and put their own needs above those of others. There was no Judgement in this World, no Reward for Being Good. Never, he said, think of anybody before you think of yourself, never offer a Hand In Help to another person, never miss a chance to stab someone in the back or kick a man when he was down, never concern yourself with the Feelings Of Others. Take what you want when you want from who you want. Always seek to gain power over others and use that power to hurt and exploit. Never be reluctant to cause damage. This, he said, is the way to Fulfilment And Happiness and a Prosperous and Successful life. When not lecturing the brothers about the wonder of wealth, the rightness of ruthlessness and the prioritization of power he would sprinkle his conversations (such as they were, for his actual interest in them was fairly limited) with the boys with what he considered to be useful 'mottos' such as:

"The value of a man is determined by how much he owns."

"The poor are poor because they are stupid. Punish them for it."

"To satisfy one's own desires at the expense of others is Divine."

"The law does not apply to the rich."

"The tears of others are as balm to your soul."

As a consequence of his philosophy of life the father had, like many bad men before and since, chosen the world of financial dealings as his preferred area of work - buying and selling commodities futures, basic foodstuffs to be precise, making much money for himself and other wealthy individuals at the price of poverty and hunger for others. After all, the poor are poor because they are stupid. Punish them for it.

Both brothers listened to the father's oft repeated advice, but not both believed it. The older brother, The Bad Brother, believed and accepted, for he was very much The Son Of The Father, handsome and intelligent, but with an air of callous ruthlessness. Had you met him, you would have felt there was certainly something a bit dark about him, a Touch Of The Troll, as it is said in the lad of Anywhere – that saying being a gross calumny against the Troll race, Trolls, in reality, being gentle and loving creatures unless called upon to protect Goodness and the harmony of the Universal Law Of Equilibrium.

The second brother, The Good Brother thought completely the opposite. He simply could not accept the father's advice; he was more The Son Of The Mother and had inherited a kind and caring nature. It was an act of Good Fortune (for the father, not the mother) that the boy's father had, by accident, married a Good Woman. This poor woman he would treat in a truly appalling fashion throughout their married life, humiliating her time and time again with his philandering, lies, abuse, violence and perversions – she staying in the marriage only because she hoped desperately to stop her boys from turning out like their repulsive father – a noble goal in which, in the case of her younger son, she was successful.

With the inevitability of the Cycle Of Life, adulthood, as evidenced by the dark hair now sprouting above their top lips, called for the brothers and, at a certain stage, they assumed full manhood (at least in the sense which society judges to be those things that make a man) and went out Into The World to Build Lives for themselves, The Bad Brother applying the philosophy of the father to all things, The Good Brother rejecting it completely and simply being caring, kind, happy-go-lucky.

And now we come to one of those points in one of my Tales from Anywhere at which you, dear Reader, expect a particular kind of ending. But, as I've said before, this is no fairy tale, this is real life and real life, like nature, is bloody in tooth and claw.

What you want me to say is that after initial success from the application of Ruthlessness And Selfishness the The Bad Brother eventually had to pay a price for his wicked ways and ended up poor, alone, a broken man, whilst The Good Brother, after some initial struggles, eventually reaped the rewards of his Kindness And Compassion, became rich, married a beautiful woman, had gorgeous children and lived happily ever after.

No. Sorry. That's not how things worked out. This is real life, remember. This is how events really unfolded...and it's a sorry story to tell.

Both brothers went into the world of business. Both being bright and hard-working, both did well. But The Bad Brother capitalised on his success and, just as the father taught, was Ruthless And Selfish, took what he wanted when he wanted and was happy to tread others into the dirt, to kick a man when he was down, to plunge a knife between the shoulder blades. He became a very, very rich man who was feared if not respected. He married a beautiful woman (who he treated like dirt just as his father had done to his mother), had gorgeous children (in whom he showed some interest but had no real love for), indulged perverse and excessive desires that ruined the lives of The Young and The Innocent. He trod all over people, used, cheated, lied, stole, damaged and raped. And had a fabulous time of it all and lived happily ever after.

The Good Brother, the Kind Compassionate One, never managed to take full advantage of his success in business; he was always thoughtful of the feelings and needs of others and never quite ruthless enough to Take The Necessary Hard Decisions. What's more, being a Kind Fellow, he was always trying to help others who found themselves in difficulty. Seeing such Kindness And Compassion, people around him (as people often do when they meet a good person) considered him to be Stupid and Foolish, not a man to be feared or regarded - so they cheated him, used him, stole from him. As a consequence of his Kindness, which others exploited as Weakness, The Good Brother would end up emotionally and financially drained, he would lose his business, his home, his family, his prospects and at the comparatively young age of 43 he would, in despair, end his life by throwing himself from a high window of The Asylum For The Strange And The Different.

And the moral of this particular tale is: The Devil really does have all the best tunes and he absolutely does look after his own.

Or does he?

Now, this is real life, remember...

And maybe I haven't been telling the whole truth?

Maybe I've been acting as journalists do, who in the land of Anywhere (just like in your own world) have long since forgotten that the duty of journalism is to search for the truth and present facts in an unbiased fashion. Instead, journalists long since came under the thrall of The Greedy One Percent (just like in your own world...), prostituting their independence and ability to think critically (or even to think) and confabulating fact and fiction to produce not news but blatant propaganda, always framed in a way that advances whatever the desired agenda of their Greedy One Percent owners/masters/pimps might be.

Maybe I'm an unreliable witness, my independence and credibility undermined by my own wish for money and influence? Maybe I'm a propaganda-peddler, not a truth-teller? Maybe I'm someone who writes for a living; in which case why the heck would you expect me to tell the truth about anything? I mean, come on, making stuff up is what I do!

Here, finally, is the real truth of real life. And it's far from plain and certainly not simple. The version of the bothers' story you have just read is indeed propaganda. It is the one told by The Greedy One Percent to their children as part of their education in how to become effective, society-killing sociopaths ready to assume their natural position in life: ruling over, and living off the blood, sweat and tears of, The Ordinary Folk.

Here is how the life (and death) of the two brothers really unfolded.

Both brothers are indeed exposed to the father's sociopathic philosophy, one does follow it, the other does not.

The Bad Brother does indeed become rich through his lifelong exercise of viciousness, but his world is essentially vacuous and loveless. Despite the trappings of wealth and the Trophy Wife his only real pleasures are the corruption of innocence, the exercise of power to destroy others and a much cherished ability to add to the Greater Sum Of Misery.

The Good Brother is indeed Kind And Caring. He never becomes rich, but neither does he Want Unduly. Those in life he is kind to do not regard him as a fool, rather as a Good Man. He lives a life full of Love And True Riches.

The Good Brother does not despair, is never incarcerated in The Asylum For The Strange And The Different and does not take his own life.

In fact, both brothers (in a bizarre, synchronicity-laden turn of events such as can only be Spun Together by the Blind Old Weaver Of Fate in her Random, Capricious Sightlessness) died of natural causes on the same day.

And so our story, the real story, begins.

Both brothers, simultaneously - to the very second - knew a sudden, sharp and all-consuming pain, mercifully short-lived, which faded away to darkness, silence, stillness. Then a burning brightness and a sensation of travel, great speed and a sweet freedom as, together, their liberated Souls travelled across the Broad, Bright. Blue Sky to That Which Lies Beyond.

Much to their surprise and bewilderment, the brothers found themselves standing in a strange, never before seen landscape. Under a leaden grey sky, a green landscape of rolling hills, occasionally marked with outcrops of grey rock or patches of thicker, taller vegetation, stretched out as far as the eye could see. Dense patches of fog rolled across the landscape like wearily patrolling soldiers and far, far in the distance rose a hill so high it seemed to be reaching for the grey sky above and atop the hill could clearly be seen a city. And it was a wondrous city, marked with high towers and of achingly beautiful construction. The city gleamed and shone, emitting a light that calmed the mind and lifted the heart. It was a Shining City On Top Of A Hill.

And the brothers turned towards each other. The Good Brother smiled and said, "brother, it's you! I've not seen you in, what, twenty years. It's a delight that we should meet again, but a shame that it's taken death to bring us together...come, let me hold you..." and The Good Brother, being a good person, moved forward with arms open to embrace his brother. But The Bad Brother, bad person that he was, backed away, "mmm, that won't be necessary, thank you, I can't say I know why we're here but I'm sure it's only temporary and I've very much removed myself from old entanglements and I have no wish to get to know you now – what would be the point, you are an Ordinary Person and you have nothing to offer me and you possess nothing I have any interest in."

What indeed would be the point? After all, a man's value is determined by what he owns, and The Bad Brother had abandoned The Good Brother two decades back, why, but why, would he want anything to do with a man who owned little, a man of no real value? Ridiculous idea! At this point the situation may have turned embarrassing were it not for a fortuitous interruption in proceedings as a persistent throat clearing sound made both brothers turn around and look behind them.

The source of the throat clearing interruption was standing there. A bored looking, somewhat Ragged And Dyspeptic Angel. "Hullo, Gentleman," said The Angel, "I'm sorry to interrupt..." at this point The Good Brother explained that that was quite alright, not a problem whilst The Bad Brother simply scowled at The Angel, which scowling caused The Angel to flap his wings once up and once down in irritation... "but I have some information to impart."

"You may have guessed by now, seeing as you both seem to have at least a modicum of intelligence," continued The Angel "that you have in fact died...for which please accept my congratulations, that whole life business can get terribly tiresome can't it? So, uh, where was I...oh yes...so, you've died and your joyfully liberated souls have sped across a Broad Blue Sky to that which etcetera etcetera...oh dear," the Angel paused, looking infinitely weary, "forgive my lack of enthusiasm, gents...do you know I've being doing this job now for six millennia...day in day out, same old spiel, same old ya-dee-da. Hummph...one would not be an Angel if one did not get a touch bored every now and then, would one?...right, sorry...you've died, okay? You got that bit? Good. Now, contrary to all that silly, religious myth nonsense that you gullible lot down there fall for hook line and sinker, getting to Heaven or, it has to be said, Hell, is not as simple as dying, being judged and ending up in one place or the other. No. Not at all. You see..." at this moment the Angel paused dramatically and then to add to the dramatic effect (for the Angel secretly yearned to be free of being a tour guide for the recently deceased and become a famous actor) he noisily and pointedly flapped his wings powerfully, once up and once down... "getting to Heaven or Hell is a more of a journey and the road to Heaven passes through..." another dramatic, nay, Shakespearian, pause... "HELL."

By this stage, both brothers were looking a bit concerned and a bit confused, taking in their looks, the Angel realized he still had a bit more explaining to do. "Okay, look, let's get this show on the road. You've both died and you are both, I'm afraid, currently standing in the outer zone of Hell or, as I prefer to call it, the Foothills Of Hell – much more poetic don't you think than 'outer zone'. I do firmly believe that we should all strive, should we not, to ensure that philosophy does not clip the wings of us Angels..." the Angel laughed at his own little pretentious literary allusion... " and over there, the big, big hill in the distance? The one with a Shining City on top? That, my friends, is Heaven. That's where you have to journey to, the place you need to reach - if you make the journey successfully then God takes it as proven that you are fit to enter His Kingdom. If you are not successful in your journey, I'm afraid you're doomed to Hell. Now, here comes the important bit, listen carefully. As we three stand here it is, at this time, morning in Hell's Foothills but in a few hours the sun – not that you can see it, the weather here in the Foothills is notoriously grim – the sun will go down and darkness will descend. When that happens, Satan's demons will spill out of Hell proper, trawling it's outer zone for any souls still there who they will drag back with them, down into the bowels of Hell and an eternity of suffering!" This dramatic announcement evinced more drama from the Angel, wings were plumped erect, chin tilted upward and arms thrown skyward.

"So that, gents, should you choose to accept it –ah hah hah hah – is your mission. Now, I suggest you get going while it's still day time. One thing...the Foothills contain certain, er, hazards that may delay or even end your journey, your ability to cope with these hazards would, mmm...might, be much helped if there are people or creatures in Heaven who are prepared to...well...you'll see what I mean. Right, off you go!"

"Can I go with my brother?" asked The Good Brother.

"No, for each soul must make it's journey through the Foothills of Hell alone. Indeed, it may interest you to know that my Angelic intuition tells me your bother doesn't want to travel with you, anyway...I'm afraid he sees you as a burden, believes he'd do far better on his own. You will go first, your brother will follow later."

"But...but..." stammered The Bad Brother, "I will have less time to make the journey than him, that's not fair!"

"Well, there you go, you shouldn't be thinking bad thoughts in front of an Angel, should you? Take it as your first lesson on the way things work in the Foothills Of Hell."

"You!" exclaimed the Angel, pointing in the direction of The Good Brother, "go now."

And The Good Brother, with one last kind (blanked and ignored) look at his sibling, started his attempt to reach Heaven, The Shining City On Top Of A Hill, taking the path that ran through The Foothills of Hell.

By and by, The Good Brother came to the first of the hazards that lie in The Foothills Of Hell: The Bog Of Evil. Coming to the top of a small, gently rising ridge, he saw before him a vast expanse of bog that he had no choice but to cross to continue his journey. How would he do that? The bog would surely suck and hold him at every step and he simply didn't have the time to spare, a delay now could be Fatal to his Mortal Soul! And as he stood there, feeling a dawning sense of hopelessness a glowing presence appeared at his side – it was another Angel! But this was one was as dramatic as the first

Angel has been dowdy, this one was a true being of Light And Beauty! As The Good Brother stared at the angelic figure in awe, it underwent a transformation: from incandescent, winged Angel to a very ordinary, friendly looking old lady, with a smile on her face, a twinkle in her eye, clutching in front of her a bulging handbag. "Hullo, my dear friend, how are you?"

"Why...why," stammered The Good Brother, "it's Irena isn't it!"

Irena had been an elderly neighbour of The Good Brother some years before his recent death. After her husband passed away she had find it difficult to make ends meet on her paltry Widows Pension (in the past these had been more generous but Irena had lived in at the time of the ascendancy of The Greedy One Percent who has systematically plundered the Public Purse and Cut Public Services to enrich themselves). The Good Brother had always been there to help her; a bit of money here, a bit of money there, an invite to 'pop round' for a bite to eat here. Irena had always felt grateful for the kindnesses of The Good Brother and remembered him fondly, even after she had made her trip to Heaven.

"I am indeed, and I am here to repay the kindness you showed me while I was alive. Remember how you would help me with money when I was desperate, even though you had little yourself?" The Good Brother shuffled his feet, smiled, looked a bit embarrassed. "Well," continued Irena, "let's see what I have in my handbag, shall we?"

Irena dug around in her bugling bag, and pulled out a thick wad of banknotes.

"Aha," she said, "money with which to repay you! Of course, money has no value here... unless...follow me!"

Irena strode determinedly off toward The Bog Of Evil and once at its edge took the bundle of notes she was holding and cast it into the bog. It landed in the damp, sucking mud and instantly swelled in size by a factor of fifty, forming a stable, floating pad upon which a person, or an Angel, could easily walk. Happily, The Good Brother joined Irena on the pad of banknotes and as he did so, she reached in her bag and pulled out another wad of money. She cast it onto the bog and it instantly swelled into a floating pad just as before. And so it went. Irena had an inexhaustible supply of wads of banknotes in her Little Old Lady handbag and in no time both she and The Good Brother had safely crossed The Bog Of Evil.

"There, my friend, Good Brother, a kindness repaid. Continue your journey now...you will find three more hazards along the way, do not despair for you are remembered with fondness in Heaven and at each hazard some person or creature will be there to help you."

Irena reached a hand up, and touched The Good Brothers cheek, and with that touch he was filled with calm and reassurance and the knowledge that Love had spun a Web Of Gossamer beneath him, to catch him should he fall. And with that, Irena faded into mist and was gone.

The Good Brother continued his journey to Heaven, The Shining City On Top Of A Hill, and, just as Irena said, he was faced with three more hazards and each at each hazard he was helped by those he had helped in his lifetime.

The next hazard was The Plain Of Shaking Stones, a flat stone plain covered with a multitude of large rocks which were violently shaking and clashing together with enough force to snap an ankle as if it were a twig. Help here came from an unusual source. In life, The Good Brother could never bring himself to step on a snail, nor leave one in a position where someone else may step on it. He would always think that, to that snail in that instance, hovering with his foot above it, deciding to crush the life out of it or not, he was like God. Given that power, The Good Brother though he should always be merciful, for surely he himself was no more than snail to God? So, each time he encountered a snail on a damp suburban pavement, The Good Brother would stop, gently pick it up and place it in a place of a safety in a nearby garden or green. And so it came to be that when he was standing before The Plain Of Shaking Stones an army of snails descended from Heaven and stormed, en masse, across the ankle destroying plain; the slimy trail of snail mucus they left in their wake solidifying and holding still the clashing rocks so that The Good Brother could easily continue his journey.

Then came The Jungle Of Impenetrable Thorns; a massive bank of vines bearing razor sharp thorns, the vines being tightly knotted together so that the only way through would be to use brute force to push your way through, tearing flesh to pieces in the process. But once again help arrived from Heaven – in the form of Edgar. Edgar was an old friend of The Good Brother. When Edgar had fallen upon hard times, The Good Brother had taken him under his wing, teaching him new knowledge and skills, mentoring him and helping him in the new career he was able to start as a result. Edgar arrived at The Jungle Of Impenetrable Thorns and showed The Good Brother that using skill, care and the right knowledge, there was a way that the thorn-laden vines could be untangled and unknotted without cutting skin and muscle to shreds. Working together they quickly untied themselves a clear path and passed safely through to the other side.

Finally, The Good Brother arrived at the last hazard, The Valley of Perpetual Darkness, a valley cloaked in a darkness so complete and so unmerciful that a man could not see a hand in front of him. Staring at the shroud of deep gloom, The Good Brother wondered what to do. He need not have feared, for there were yet friends of his in Heaven. And Daniel appeared. Daniel, another friend of The Good Brother's, who had experienced a period in his life when he had descended into a deep depression which had cloaked him in a dark blanket of misery, despair, hopelessness. But The Good Brother was There For Him. Always with a friendly word, always with encouragement, always with support, always ready to listen without judging, a light to help show the way, and gradually Daniel had emerged from his own Valley of Perpetual Darkness.

Daniel took The Good Brother by the hand and led him into The Valley of Perpetual Darkness, but as soon as its gloom enfolded the two of them, Daniel glowed with a bright, angelic light and lit the way so that The Good Brother quickly and safely passed to the other side of The Valley of Perpetual Darkness.

And so it was that The Good Brother made a safe and successful journey through the The Foothills Of Hell to arrive at the base of that hill, the hill atop of which stood the shining City of Heaven.

But the hill was high, and oh so steep. How would he climb it? How, but how could he climb it? But he need not have feared, for once again the Gates Of Heaven opened to let pass one of its residents. Suddenly at The Good Brother's feet was Donkey. Donkey was, in fact, not a donkey but a dog, his beloved, shaggy, mongrel dog. The first dog that had come into his life to (as dogs do) teach him of love when he arrived and of loss when he left. The Good Brother had always loved Donkey dearly and had always treated him like a Prince, walking him, feeding him, caring for him. Now Donkey was here to Repay The Favour.

Donkey looked up at his master, smiled (in a doggy way) and barked and a pack of Joyful Dogs emerged from behind a nearby small hillock and sprinted up to The Good Brother.

The pack consisted of three powerful and large Alsatians, two feisty Jack Russells and five elegant Dachshunds. The Alsatians moved in close to each other, side by side, packed together. The Dachshunds jumped on top of the Alsatians and climbed one on top of the other, facing alternate ways and across the broad backs of the Alsatians whilst the two Jack Russells jumped up and stood on either side, facing forward. They had formed a chair. A chair of dogs. But not just a chair, this was a throne. A Throne Of Dogs.

With a bark of encouragement from Donkey, The Good Brother sat down on this wonderful, living, strange Throne Of Dogs, buttocks resting on the Alsatians, back resting against the stack of Dachshunds and arms lying either side upon the Jack Russells.

And Donkey began to run, to run like the wind, Barking Joyously and closely followed by the Throne Of Dogs and its human occupant, swiftly carrying The Good Brother up the steep Hill, to the gleaming City, to Heaven itself.

So what, then happened to The Bad Brother? You mean you've not guessed yet? Extraordinary. In that case, I'd better tell you, hadn't I?

What happens next – what happens to the bad brother...buy the book and find out!